ANIMAL
ALERT

SKIN AND BONE

Animal Alert series

ANIMAL
ALERT

SKIN AND BONE

Jenny Oldfield

Hodder
Children's
Books

a division of Hodder Headline plc

Special thanks to Sue Reddington, Tony Lane and Sandy
Middleton of Meanwood Valley Urban Farm.
Thanks also to David Brown and Margaret Marks of Leeds
RSPCA Animal Home and Clinic, and to Raj Duggal M.V.Sc.,
M.R.C.V.S. and Louise Kinvig B.V.M.S., M.R.C.V.S.

First published in Great Britain in 1998
by Hodder Children's Books

British Library Cataloguing in Publication Data
A record for this book is available from the British Library

ISBN 0 340 70878 6

Typeset by Avon Dataset Ltd, Bidford-on-Avon, Warks

Printed and bound in Great Britain by
Mackays of Chatham plc, Chatham, Kent

Hodder and Stoughton
A division of Hodder Headline plc
338 Euston Road
London NW1 3BH

Foreword

Tess, my eight-year-old border collie, has been injured by a speeding car. I rush her to the vet's. The doors of the operating theatre swing open, a glimpse of bright lights and gleaming instrument, then, 'Don't worry, we'll do everything we can for her,' a kind nurse promises, shepherding me away . . .

Road traffic accidents, stray dogs, sad cases of cruelty and neglect: spend a day in any busy city surgery and watch the vets and nurses make their vital, split-second decisions. If, like me, you've ever owned or longed to own an animal, you'll admire as much as I do the work of these dedicated people. And you'll know from experience exactly what the owners in my *Animal Alert* stories are going through. Luckily for me, Tess came safely through her operation, but endings aren't always so happy . . .

Jenny Oldfield
19 March 1997

1

'Hold his tail down and lift his leg!' Liz Hutchins ordered. 'Go on, Carly. George won't bite.'

'No, but he might kick.' Carly Grey didn't fancy a hoof the size of a dinner plate landing in the pit of her stomach.

George was a shire horse, on loan to Sedgewood City Farm from a nearby brewery. He'd gone lame in his back leg and Geoff Best, the farm manager, had called the vets at Beech Hill for help.

'That's why I'm telling you to hold his tail

down,' Liz explained. She stood calmly at the front end of the giant grey horse, holding his head collar and stroking his velvety nose. 'If you do that, a horse is unlikely to kick out at you.'

So Carly seized a bunch of wiry white hair in one hand and bent forward to lift the leg with the other. George snorted a cloud of steamy breath into the frosty air, shunted sideways and pinned her against the wall.

'Ouch!' The lame foot and what felt like several tons of solid horseflesh landed on her toes.

'One lame horse plus one lame assistant.' Liz grinned and came to take over. 'Go on, you grab his head while I try to find out what's wrong with him.'

Gratefully Carly hobbled out of the danger zone. Her toes throbbed as she took hold of the collar and felt George's hot breath on her face. 'Good boy,' she murmured, patting his massive neck. She wondered why she'd come to the farm with Liz instead of heading straight for school.

'Sound as if you mean it.' Liz was already at

work. She lifted the hoof and rested its weight between her knees to inspect the underside.

'There, good boy!' *I could have been in B Hall in the warmth, waiting for the registration bell,* she thought. *Instead of standing in the freezing cold, being trampled on by a cart-horse!*

'That's more like it.' Liz scraped at the horny part of the hoof with a knife. 'There's nothing wrong with the foot, so it must be the leg,' she decided. She ran an expert hand over the fetlock and knee joint, shook her head.

'Good boy, George!' Carly hung on to the collar, knowing that if this mountain of a horse decided to break free, she wouldn't be able to do a thing about it. Cats, yes. Dogs, rabbits and guinea-pigs, no problem. She was fine with all the small animals that came into the surgery at Beech Hill. She could even help during operations when her father, Paul Grey, and Liz needed her, and she never flinched. But her heart was in her mouth as she stared up at the rolling eyes and flared nostrils of the lame cart-horse.

'Ah!' Liz's fingers probed through the long hair covering the ankle. 'See this swelling here, just above the hoof? This part of the leg is called the pastern. If it's swollen, it could mean a condition called ringbone. It's where a knock or a sprain jars the joint and causes an extra piece of bone to form.'

'Is it serious?' Carly felt the horse quiver with pain.

'He may be permanently lame.' Liz put the hoof down on the stable floor to see how George held the foot. 'On the other hand, the swelling could be caused by cracks in his heel, see?'

Carly nodded. Her fingers were frozen, her knuckles white, but still she held on.

'In which case, at some point his heels and legs have been covered in mud, and there's been an irritant in the soil, which has made a sore patch that's grown septic and swollen. Yes, that's more likely to be it!' Liz fetched a plastic tub from her bag.

'And that's not so serious?' Carly trusted Liz to know what she was talking about. Though she was a young vet, recently out of college, Carly's dad had taken Liz on at Beech Hill because she was especially skilled with large animals. She'd grown up on a farm in

Scotland, and still liked dealing with horses, cattle and sheep. That was why he'd sent her to Sedgewood when they'd got the call.

'Nope. It just needs a dab of zinc oxide every now and then.' Once more she lifted the giant foot to smear the white ointment over the heel. 'Geoff Best will be relieved when we tell him. How's your foot?' she asked, finishing with the ointment and glancing at her watch.

'OK. Pretty sore, but I don't think anything's broken.'

'Good. You can let go of his head now. Come on, we'd better pack up here and get you over to school.' Brisk and satisfied with her diagnosis, Liz went to tell the farm manager the good news while Carly hopped and hobbled into the yard.

Outside, in the early January morning, she took a quick look round at the ducks huddled in the shelter of a narrow wooden bridge over a half-frozen stream.

Sedgewood Farm was in the middle of the city, but you would hardly have guessed it. Carly could only just see the outline of high-rise flats on the dark hill beyond the sweep of fields and bare hedges in the narrow valley. In the half-light she could make out a small flock of hardy sheep on the frozen hillside, a bare vegetable garden nearer to the farm buildings, then a wooden barn where they kept the cows in winter, and next to that a noisy hen-house. In the yard where Carly stood, there was a block of redbrick buildings made into a shop, a café and an office. Opposite this was the row of stables where George had planted his great hoof on her foot.

'That's right; rest the leg and apply the ointment a couple of times a day.' Liz came hurrying out of the office followed by a short man with a beard, wearing a battered green jacket and a navy polo-necked sweater. 'If it doesn't improve by tomorrow, try a poultice with dry warm bran over the affected area. Wrap the bandage tight, OK?' She flung her bag into the back of her ancient sports car and told Carly to hop in.

'Huh!' She couldn't do anything *except* hop!

'Sorry, I forgot!' Liz jumped in herself. 'Give me a call if you're still worried,' she told Geoff Best.

'Thanks.' He came and leaned his arm along the soft top of the car, then peered in through the steamy window. 'Er, about your bill . . .'

'That's OK. We won't send you an invoice until the end of the month,' Liz said breezily. She started the engine. 'There's no hurry.'

The farm manager looked relieved. 'Thanks. I hadn't reckoned on George going lame on us. It's been a bad month for bills. We had to buy extra feed because of the cold weather, and we had a frozen water pipe burst on us last week, not to mention the council threatening to take away our grant next year!' He managed a wry smile.

'It sounds bad.'

'Could be better,' he agreed. 'Anyway, thanks for coming. You've set my mind at rest.'

He watched them drive out over the bridge, past the barn and the hen-house. Carly waved, then settled in for the journey across the city; through rows of terraced houses on to underpasses that tunnelled under the heart of the city, on to the ring road towards Beech Hill. *Throb-throb* went her foot, her fingers tingled as they warmed up under the blast from the heater. Her nose twitched and tickled. 'Aatchoo!'

'Bless you!' Liz drew up outside Morningside Comprehensive. Bells were already ringing and the last kids were scurrying across the playground. 'You'll just make it if you run along.'

'Huh!' she said again, with feeling. She took her schoolbag from the boot and limped away.

'Oops!' This time Liz laughed out loud. 'You'll get no sympathy from me, Carly Grey! We vets often have to suffer for our vocation. Getting stamped on is only one small hazard of the job!'

'. . . Don't tell me; you've been nursing some poor animal back to health!' Carly's group tutor, Mr Howell, was used to the vet's daughter showing up at the last minute looking breathless and dishevelled.

Every head in the room swivelled towards her.

'Sort of.' She sat at her desk, head down, red in the face. 'Sorry I'm late,' she muttered.

The teacher marked her present and closed

the register. He scanned the room for an unwilling messenger. 'Jon, take this along to the office for me, please.'

Carly's friend, Hoody, scowled from the back row near the door. He hated it when teachers used his real name. So he lurched out of his seat and shuffled forward to the front desk. He was about to grab the register when Mr Howell stopped him.

'Is this your version of correct school uniform?' he said in a bad-tempered voice, looking Hoody up and down.

Carly frowned and made a face at Hanna Walsh in the next row.

'Which side of bed did *he* get out of?' Hanna whispered, daringly loud. The rest of the class had stopped gossiping and tuned in to Hoody and the group tutor.

Hoody looked his usual self: his trainers were scuffed, his crumpled white shirt wasn't tucked into his grey trousers, his collar was open and his cropped brown hair was standing up on end.

'Where's your tie?' Mr Howell demanded. He was dressed in the same fawn shirt, brown knitted tie, and baggy tweed jacket he'd worn for generations.

Out came the tie from Hoody's pocket, limp and creased. His scowl deepened.

'You know the rule.' The teacher waited with over-the-top, fake patience until Hoody slung it round his neck. 'That's better.' At last he released the register, Hoody took it and the class relaxed.

As Hoody slunk past her desk with it, Carly gave him a sympathetic smile. *Never mind about Howler; we all know what he's like.* Then another bell went and there was a scramble for the door. She grabbed her bag and joined the scrum, heading for double maths.

'Carly!' A voice muttered at her elbow as she passed the office.

She was with Hanna and another friend, Cleo. They all turned at the sound of Hoody's voice.

'What?' Trying not to go red only made you go a deeper shade of crimson, she realised. Hoody never, *ever* talked to girls in school. He didn't even talk to other boys much.

'Can you meet me after school?'

Hanna nudged Cleo and giggled. They hung

back against the wall, staring at Hoody with big smirks on their faces.

'What for?'

'I'll tell you later. Can you?'

'Where?'

'By the railway behind Hillman's super-market.' He did his best to ignore the goggling audience.

'What time?' Carly couldn't believe that tough Hoody would be seen dead fixing a time and a place to meet her. Usually he drifted round school as if he didn't even know her.

'Four o'clock.'

'I'm not sure if I can make it.' She'd promised her dad she would go straight home from school to help in the surgery.

Hoody's face clamped shut. His eyes nar-rowed, he screwed up his mouth. 'OK, forget it.' He turned on his heel and bumped straight into a gang of sixth-formers in the crowded corridor.

'No, wait!' Carly darted after him. 'Make it half four. Give me time to go home first, then I'll be able to make it. Do you mean that patch of waste ground?'

He nodded and shrugged. 'But I said forget it, OK?'

'I'll be there at half four,' she promised. She knew it must be important.

Another nod and he was off, lost in the crowd.

'*Très* romantic!' Cleo giggled. ' "Meet me on the rubbish tip behind the supermarket!" ' She and Hanna bundled Carly off towards maths.

'It's not like that,' she insisted.

'Oh no?' they teased. 'What *is* it like then?'

'I've no idea!' Carly strode off. Well, one idea, actually. Knowing Hoody, this after-school meeting had something to do with animals. That's what Carly and he had in common: waifs and strays, cats, dogs, horses, rabbits, birds and hamsters.

2

It was dark by four o'clock, and snowing as Carly made her way home to Beech Hill. The traffic was at a standstill, churning out exhaust fumes, as cars and buses got bogged down in the slush.

'Lovely day!' Bupinda greeted her from behind her desk in reception. The waiting room was crowded with patients; the usual dogs and cats with sniffs and snuffles, or needing jabs, X-rays, dressings or dental work.

Carly sighed and unzipped her jacket. 'Where's Dad?'

'In Room 1. You should see what he's got in there with him!' The receptionist made it sound special.

So Carly ditched her schoolbag behind the desk and headed straight for the treatment room.

'Hi, Carly. Come and take a look at this.' Paul Grey glanced over his shoulder.

'*Eee-aaagh!*' There was a blood-curdling screech from the creature on the table.

She jumped. What on earth was it? The owner of whatever it was stood frowning at the far side of the table. He was a middle-aged man in a leather jacket with a chunky gold watch on his wrist and grey hair slicked back over his balding head. He chewed the edge of his thumbnail as he watched Paul Grey at work.

'OK, now if you stand back out of his line of vision, he might settle down a bit,' Carly's dad suggested.

'*Eee-aaagh!*' The creature screeched again.

'Is it a parrot?' Carly moved round for her first glimpse. A big red bird with blue and yellow wings pecked at Paul Grey's hand with his powerful hooked beak. He sat on a perch inside a battered wire cage, feathers ruffled, chained by the leg.

'No, not quite. It's a macaw.' Gingerly her dad put his hand inside the cage. The bird darted its head at him, missed, and rattled his beak against the bar. Paul Grey had whipped his hand back just in time. 'You don't see too many of these. He's magnificent, isn't he?'

Carly crept closer, uneasy under the bird's fierce gaze. 'What's his name?' she asked the owner.

'Mac.' The answer was blunt and ended with a sniff.

'Mac's pulling out some of the feathers on his chest.' Paul Grey pointed through the bars to show her. 'It can be a sign that the bird is lonely and doesn't have enough space,' he told the man. 'Do you let him out of the cage?'

'I only got him last week. They never told me I was meant to let him out.' Another sniff as he wrinkled his nose in a nervous tic.

'Was he chained up like this when you bought him?'

The man nodded. He backed towards the

door uneasily. 'Can you do anything for him? Only it doesn't look good, and that bald patch is getting bigger by the day.'

'*Eea-aagh!*' Mac screeched angrily. He spread his wings so that the tips touched the sides of the cage.

'Where did you say you'd bought him?' Paul Grey stood well back, looking thoughtful.

'I didn't. From a friend.' Sniff, twitch, more backing out of the door. 'Look, if it's going to be expensive to put him right, don't bother. I'll just take him back to this friend of mine, tell him I want a different one. He can get hold of all sorts of colours if I ask him to.'

By now Carly's dad was frowning deeply. 'You know there are regulations controlling the import of exotic birds?'

The man was practically out of the door. 'It means nothing to me,' he protested. 'I bought him off a friend, that's all.' He was gone, out of sight, rushing through reception. It was the mention of regulations that had done it.

Paul Grey would have gone after him if this hadn't been the moment Mac chose to make his own bid for freedom. He squawked noisily, beat his wings against his sides, and launched himself from his dirty perch. The chain on his leg pulled tight and sent him fluttering to the floor of the cage.

'Poor thing!' Carly cried. Helpless and frustrated, the macaw floundered in the dirt.

Her dad seized his chance. Grabbing a towel and wrapping it round the macaw, he managed to pinion the bird's wings to its sides. 'We'll have to clip through the chain with wire cutters,' he told Carly. 'Can you see if Steve has got some in the van?'

She ran to find Steve Winter, the animal inspector at Beech Hill.

'He's in the kennels,' Bupinda told her, 'checking out injuries to the cruelty case we're keeping in isolation.'

So she ran again, to the kennel block at the back of the Rescue Centre, and found Steve talking to Liz about the mongrel dog's broken ribs. She burst in and asked for the tool from the van. 'We've got a macaw chained to its perch! You should see it, it can hardly move. It's really cruel!'

Steve handed her the key to the van. 'The

wire cutters are in the toolbox in the back. Tell
your dad I'll be along in a minute.' He was on
the case in a flash. 'Sounds like the owner
needs a word or two of advice about how to
look after his pet.'

'Too late. He already left in a big hurry.'
Carly was dashing back to reception, through
the main door into the carpark. By the time she
found the tool and got back to the treatment
room, Steve was already there, looking on as
Paul Grey examined the poor condition of the
macaw.

'This feather plucking is typical,' her dad explained. He handled the macaw gently, pointing out the bare patch of skin on its chest. 'It
indicates bad diet and boredom from being
cooped up; a whole range of problems.' He
took the wire cutters from Carly and deftly
snipped through a link in the chain. Then he
was able to lift the bird out of the cage.

Steve looked thoughtful. 'I'm wondering if
it's been brought into the country illegally,' he
murmured. 'You say the owner's only had it
for a week?'

'According to him.' Paul let Carly stroke the

macaw's crimson feathers with her little finger. The bird had quietened down under the careful attention they were giving him. 'It could have been shipped in from abroad fairly recently.'

'Smuggled, more like.' Steve considered what they should do. 'In which case, he's skipped quarantine regulations.'

'Carly, could you go and give Liz a hand in Room 2?' Bupinda's voice over the intercom broke into the conversation. 'And bring a cat basket with you.'

Carly left her dad and Steve to make a decision about the macaw. She was off on her evening flurry of activity, taking patients upstairs to the overnight cattery, wiping down treatment tables, feeding the dogs in the kennels at the back. For two hours she was run off her feet, and when surgery finally finished and she could crawl upstairs to the flat where she and her father lived, she was worn out.

She closed the door behind her, kicked off her shoes and flopped on to the sofa. Her eyes were shut as she soaked up the silence of the empty flat, then she felt light paws tread across her, and sharp little claws pull on her school jumper. 'Hello, Ruby!' she opened her eyes to see Beech Hill's small tortoiseshell cat.

Ruby purred and rubbed her face against Carly's.

'OK, you're hungry, I know!' She glanced at her watch. Ten past six. 'Oh no!' She sat bolt upright, sending Ruby scampering to the floor.

'What is it?' Paul Grey came yawning into the room. He took off his white coat and slung it across a chair.

'Hoody! I was meant to meet him an hour and a half ago. I completely forgot!' She jumped to her feet, looking round for her jacket.

'Whoa! You're not going anywhere!' Her dad stood by the door. 'There's six inches of snow out there, in case you didn't realise!'

Carly dashed to the window and looked out at a strange white world. Snowflakes whirled in the light of the streetlamps, and the snow had covered roads, roofs and trees with a thick, pure white layer. 'But I promised I'd be there!' she protested.

'Forget it, Carly,' Paul Grey insisted. He went through to the kitchen to begin cooking supper.

'So, you forgot. It happens. And whatever it was can't have been that important. If it was, Hoody would have called here to find you.'

This made sense, Carly knew. But she was uneasy. And all through the evening – as she set the table for supper and washed up afterwards, as she watched television and got ready for bed – she still felt bad about letting Hoody down.

'If it hadn't been important, he'd never have asked me to meet him in the first place,' she told herself. Hoody was like that; a kind of semi-detached kid who never asked favours in case you let him down.

And now she had done exactly that. She'd failed to show up. Full stop. There was no getting away from it. She pictured him waiting for her in the snow by the railway line, imagined his thin, scowling face as he realised she wasn't going to come. He would turn up the collar of his denim jacket, shove his hands in his pockets and shuffle off. Next time he saw her he probably wouldn't even speak to her.

'What's the betting he won't give me a chance to say I'm sorry?' she whispered to

Ruby, snuggled up on the bed beside her. 'And I really am, if he only knew!'

'This is an odd one!' Mel, the nurse at the Rescue Centre, was putting down the phone in reception early next morning just as Carly came downstairs. She wrote something on a notepad. 'I've just had a call from a man using a mobile phone. He says he's sitting on a stationary train by Hillman's, watching a boy mistreating a donkey, of all things!'

'A donkey?' Liz was on duty. 'What's a donkey doing near a railway line in the middle of a city?'

'Exactly. In this weather too!'

Carly overheard the conversation as she went to pick up the mail from the mat. A boy? A railway line? She began to pay more attention.

'According to the guy on the phone, the poor donkey's a bag of bones, and the kid has tied a rope around his neck and is trying to pull him along.'

Liz clicked her tongue in annoyance. 'I'm due to start surgery in ten minutes. Better get

Steve along there straight away. Tell him to take the trailer.'

'He's not in yet. He's calling in on Bill Brookes at the pet shop on City Road to see if he's heard anything on the grapevine about this illegal macaw we've got upstairs.'

'How long will he be?' Liz made it clear that this sounded like an emergency that couldn't wait.

'About half an hour.'

'That could be too late. The kid will probably have gone by the time he gets there.'

'I could go on ahead.' Carly spoke quietly. 'I'll cut across the main road and down by the allotments to the railway.' Something told her she should. 'At least I'll be able to give Steve a description if I get there before him.'

Quickly Liz nodded. 'OK, but stay out of trouble. Wait for Steve to get there before you do anything.' She told Mel to divert their inspector from the pet shop straight to the scene of the incident.

Meanwhile, Carly braced herself to face the outside world. What had been a white wonderland the night before had quickly changed to a nightmare of dirty snow piled up by ploughs at the roadsides. The pavements were solid ice – deathtraps for unwary shoppers and nervous old ladies.

The quickest way was to walk on the road, she decided. There wasn't much traffic up Beech Hill, and cars on the main road went at a slow crawl. She crossed to the central reservation, saw a gang of kids on the corner by the Black Bull pub, changed course and headed towards them. 'Hi, have you seen Hoody?' she asked anxiously.

'Why do you want to know?' Cleo Morris was in the group, standing there with a smirk on her face.

'Have you?' Carly ignored her. She didn't have time to mess around.

'Not since school yesterday,' a boy said. 'No one's seen him.'

She nodded and went on down King Edward's Road. It was the answer she'd been expecting. Round a bend, out of sight, a train rattled by. Carly skidded on some ice, felt her foot begin to throb again and clung on to a lamppost. But she had to get a move on.

Testing her foot on the ground, she made her way more slowly down the hill.

At last she came to the flat land between the supermarket carpark and the railway. The rail company used it to shunt unwanted carriages into sidings and for storing heaps of grey stone chippings inside concrete bunkers. Local kids ignored the KEEP OUT notices to climb through the barbed wire fence and spray graffiti on every bit of wall space.

Today, though, in the grimy snow, it seemed deserted. Carly's footprints were the first to cross the wide open space. Or so she thought. There was an abandoned row of goods trucks up ahead, and, beyond that, a patch of freshly scuffed and trampled snow. She ducked down to look under the rusty wheels for a better view.

The first thing she saw was a pair of scruffy trainers and frayed jeans. Then more legs, with hooves that flailed and kicked up lumps of frozen snow. She heard a donkey bray and a boy's voice urging it to move.

Carly came round the end of the goods truck. 'Hoody!' She couldn't believe it. There he was tugging at a frayed piece of blue rope attached to a head collar on the most pathetic creature she thought she'd ever seen.

The donkey was skeleton thin. His ribs stuck out through his dark brown coat, his hip bones practically poked through his skin. His poor legs were knock-kneed, his shaggy mane was matted with frost and dirt.

'Stop it! What are you doing?' She ran forward over the rough, churned-up snow.

'What's it look like?' Hoody snapped without bothering to turn round. Instead, he kept hold of the rope and pulled.

'It looks like you're being cruel on purpose!' She was yelling at him to make him stop. The rope was fastened to a frayed head collar that cut into the donkey's face.

'What do you want me to do? Leave him here to freeze to death?'

'Where are you trying to take him?' In her panic, Carly grabbed hold of Hoody's arm.

He shoved her sideways. 'Into this truck, where do you think?'

One side of the disused wagon had been smashed out and lowered to make a wobbly ramp. There was a pile of newspapers stacked inside and a plastic carrier bag full of what looked like hay.

'But you can't force him!' She saw the donkey dig in his heels. The collar cut deeper into the sore patch on his cheek.

'He's gonna die if I leave him here much longer!' Suddenly Hoody stopped tugging. He let the rope hang loose as he sagged forward. 'He's been out all night in the freezing cold. Look at him, he's skin and bone!'

Carly understood now what Hoody's plan was. He'd brought food, made the crude ramp, and was trying to line the truck with newspaper to keep the donkey warm. 'Is this what you wanted to show me last night?'

He grunted. 'I knew I'd have trouble trying to shift him into the shelter by myself.'

'How did he get here?' She looked again at the trembling, starving creature.

'Search me. Someone left him tied up to that post. I saw him on my way to school yesterday morning.'

'He's been here all this time?' In the sub-zero temperature, all through a long, dark night. It was a miracle he'd survived this long, she knew. 'OK, but you can't pull and shove him into the truck. You have to get him to co-operate.' Carly clicked into action. She ran up the ramp to grab a handful of hay from the bag.

'What are you doing here anyway?' For the first time Hoody looked her full in the face. He had his back to the donkey, standing hands on hips with the rope wrapped loosely round his wrist.

'We got a phone call at Beech Hill. Someone saw you from a train. Steve's on his way. I came on ahead.' She came slowly down the ramp, determined to tempt the donkey out of the biting cold. 'Why didn't you come and tell us last night?'

'I was waiting here for you, wasn't I?' He backed away to let her by. 'I didn't want to leave him by himself after it started snowing.' Stepping backwards, he missed his footing and slipped.

The sudden action tugged the rope taut. The donkey's head jerked and he whinnied in pain. His hooves trampled in the snow close to Hoody's head.

'Watch out!' Carly cried. She dropped the hay and ran down the ramp.

Hoody tried to roll sideways, but his body got caught in the rope. The donkey's feet thudded closer.

Carly saw Hoody raise his arms to cover his head. She saw the donkey rear up. His head jerked as the collar cut into his flesh, then he brought his hooves down on top of the figure rolling on the ground.

3

The starving creature used his last ounce of strength to stagger out of sight.

Carly dropped to her knees beside Hoody. From what she knew about helping animals at the scene of an accident, she realised she must not move him. He lay unconscious, but still breathing, curled up with his knees against his chest, one arm crooked over his head. She couldn't see his face, but she noticed his ribs moving up and down as he drew breath.

She must keep him warm. Quickly she unzipped her jacket and put it over him. As she tried to tuck it under his body, her fingers came into contact with the warm, sticky feel of blood. To her horror, as she drew them away, she saw they were stained red.

Stop the bleeding! she told herself. She could see it now, seeping across the snow from a cut at the back of Hoody's neck where the donkey's hoof must have caught him. She needed to make a pad to press against the wound, so she took off her scarf and folded it, held it hard in place, trying not to move the injured body. Then she looked up.

Where was the donkey now? As another train rattled along the track fifty metres away, she caught a movement beyond one of the concrete bunkers, and she saw him shy and stagger farther off, still trailing the blue rope. He zig-zagged here and there across the derelict yard: a walking skeleton, hardly aware of where he was or what was happening.

And then, thank heavens, she heard a car cruising along the rim of the supermarket car-park, and she spotted the Beech Hill van, driven by Steve. 'Over here!' Scared to take the wedge of scarf away from Hoody's neck, she yelled, 'Steve, we're here, come quick!'

For a few seconds she thought he hadn't heard. The van was towing a trailer that clattered over the heaps of shovelled snow. But Steve was driving with his window down, half-leaning out and scanning the area of waste ground by the railway track. He saw Carly crouched over a body lying in the snow.

'OK, I can see you!' He jumped out and ran to the wire fence. 'What happened?'

'It's Hoody! He's unconscious and bleeding. Ring for an ambulance, Steve!' She glanced down as Hoody's arm flopped clear of his face. His eyes were closed, his skin deathly pale. Her cream-coloured scarf was soaked through with crimson blood.

By the time Steve had called the emergency services, wrenched open a gate in the fence and come running to help, Hoody was beginning to come round. His eyelids flickered, he moved his head, then he slumped back.

'Don't move!' Carly whispered. She was terrified that the blows from the donkey's hooves had hurt his neck or bones lower down his spine.

Hoody's eyes flickered again. He groaned.

'Keep him still!' Steve yelled as he ran, slipping and skidding across the snow. He was tearing off his own jacket, ready to use it as a blanket when he arrived. He dropped down beside them, just as Hoody opened his eyes properly for the first time. 'It's OK, just don't move!' Steve warned him. 'The ambulance is on its way.'

Hoody lay quiet. He tried to say something, so Carly leaned forward to make out the words.

'What's he say?' Steve had taken the blood-soaked pad from her and started to use proper dressings from the bag he'd grabbed from the van.

'He's asking about the donkey.' She explained what had happened. 'Listen, Hoody, don't worry about that right now, OK?'

'Where? Bones? Did you – is he – in the truck?' His words tumbled out again, slurred and jumbled.

'Bones is OK,' she lied. 'Don't think about him. We've got to get you to hospital!' She felt as if her heart was in her throat and choking her, tears came to her eyes. Hoody's voice didn't sound like him at all.

'Here comes the ambulance now!' Steve picked up the siren in the distance. 'Stay here, Carly! Hold this dressing in place.' He was on his feet, running to show the paramedics the way across the bleak ground.

'Vinny!' Hoody mumbled. He tried to raise his head.

Vinny was Hoody's mongrel. The two went everywhere together.

'He's not here. Isn't he at home?' She hadn't seen any sign of the tough little dog.

'Ran off – wouldn't stop – donkey!' Hoody murmured. 'Vinny!'

She thought she understood. 'What are you saying? You brought Vinny with you, but the donkey scared him off?'

He gave a faint nod, then closed his eyes.

Steve and two paramedics in green uniforms were running back with a stretcher and more medical aid.

'Don't worry. Vinny probably went straight back home to Beacon Street.' She tried to reassure him. 'He wouldn't go far.'

Hoody sighed and groaned.

Then the paramedics took over, quickly testing his reflexes before they covered him with a foil blanket and began to lift him expertly and swiftly on to the stretcher. 'Has anyone rung his parents?' one asked, as they picked Hoody up and carried him.

'He doesn't live with them. He lives with his sister,' Carly told them. She ran to keep up. 'She's not on the phone.'

'Vinny.' Hoody was faintly repeating his dog's name over and over.

'Can someone tell his sister?' the woman paramedic asked. They'd reached the ambulance where a small crowd of early Saturday morning shoppers had gathered.

Steve glanced at Carly. 'I'll drive in the ambulance to the hospital. Can you run up to Beacon Street?'

She hesitated. 'What about Hoody?' She wanted to know that he was going to be OK.

'You did well, Carly. But let's leave it to the experts now. The best thing for you to do is to let his sister know what's happened.' Steve climbed in after the stretcher.

'Vinny!' Hoody whispered.

So Carly leaned into the ambulance. 'It's OK, don't worry about Vinny. I'll find him for you,' she promised, sure that the sensible dog had headed home. Hoody was already hooked up to drips and tubes. There was an oxygen mask over his face to help him breathe.

'Tell his sister to come straight to the hospital!' Steve warned, as the door slammed shut. 'St Mark's A and E Department!'

Carly swallowed hard. The ambulance engine whined as the tyres slid over the icy surface, then gripped. The blue light flashed and the siren began to wail, as the crowd of onlookers stepped back.

With a big effort she pushed the picture of Hoody's deathly white face, his dark, dazed eyes, from her mind. Then she turned and ran from the patch of bloodstained ground.

Zoe Hood opened her front door and took one look at Carly's pale, staring face. 'It's Hoody, isn't it?'

Carly nodded. 'He's had an accident. They've taken him to hospital!'

'How bad?' Zoe snatched her leather jacket from the hook in the hall. She yelled back down the corridor to tell her boyfriend, Dean, the news.

'They don't know yet. He was unconscious, but he was coming round when they took him off in the ambulance.' She gasped and held on to the doorpost, straining for sounds of a dog in the kitchen at the end of the corridor. 'He was asking for Vinny. Is he here?'

'No. They both went out early. I haven't seen either of them since.' Zoe scrambled for change for the bus-fare in the pockets of her jacket. 'I knew it was trouble the moment I saw you!' She ran a hand decorated with heavy silver rings through her short brown hair.

Then Dean appeared, still sleepy and un-shaven in T-shirt and jeans. He grumbled about Zoe having to go off before she'd made his breakfast. 'What's up? Has he been in a fight or what?' he asked Carly.

'No. He's been kicked. He was trying to rescue a starving donkey and it reared up and hit him.'

Dean swore and turned back. 'Stupid kid.'

As Zoe stepped out on to Beacon Street, Carly tried to call her boyfriend back. 'Hoody's worried about Vinny. I promised to find him. Are you sure he didn't come home?'

'No. Stupid dog.' Dean was in no mood to help. 'He needn't expect me to look after it while they keep him in the hospital!' He slammed the door behind him.

So Carly ran along the pavement after Zoe. 'When you get there, will you tell Hoody that I'm still looking for Vinny?' she urged. Part of her wanted to go with Zoe to see how Hoody was, to get on the bus that was lurching over the snow towards the bus stop. But she knew she couldn't do that until she'd tracked down his beloved dog. 'Tell him he can't have gone far and not to worry!'

She yelled the last four words as Hoody's sister stepped up into the bus. As the door hissed shut, Carly stood and watched it ease back into the traffic, feeling her heart thud with anxiety.

It was one thing sending a message to Hoody not to worry, another thing to take her own advice. How was she going to find the runaway dog? And if she didn't find Vinny, Hoody would be heartbroken. Then there was the donkey. Hoody had christened him Bones, and the name stuck. Where had Bones staggered off to after he'd reared up and injured Hoody? How much longer could he last in this cold, without food or shelter? Who would come looking with her?

Carly glanced at her watch. It was only half past nine. Surgery at Beech Hill would still be in full swing. Saturday was their busiest day. No one there would be free to go searching for a mistreated donkey. The best plan was to wait until Steve got away from the hospital and came back to Hillman's to collect the van and trailer. That might be in about an hour. Until then she should scour the streets and the park for Vinny. When she found him, it would be one piece of good news to pass on to poor Hoody.

So she retraced her steps to the supermarket, asking everyone she knew the same question.

'Have you seen Hoody's dog?'

Each time she got the same answer, and a question.

'No. Why, what's happened?'

'Hoody's been hurt. He's in hospital. Vinny ran off and disappeared.' Carly's explanation spread like wildfire. By the time she reached City Road, kids were running up to her to ask how he was.

'I heard he broke his neck!' they whispered, eyes wide, breath pouring out in clouds into the freezing air. 'They say he can't move his arms and legs!' or, 'He's bleeding to death, isn't he? They can't find the right blood in the blood bank. Hoody's got a rare type; that's what I heard.'

'I don't know!' Carly could hardly bear to hear it. What she wanted to know was had they seen Vinny?

But no one had, and still the rumours spread.

'Hoody got kicked in the head, didn't he? His skull's smashed and now he's on a life-support machine. They don't think he's gonna make it!'

She ran on, away from the gossip, back down to the railway yard. She climbed a broken-down part of the fence and searched in the bunkers, under the old trucks. 'Vinny.

Here, boy!' She shouted and whistled, but the yard felt deserted. A wind blew along the silent track and gusted up clouds of powdery snow. Carly shivered. For the first time she remembered she'd given Hoody her jacket – then she saw her bloody scarf lying discarded on the trampled ground where the accident had happened. Footprints, the marks of a donkey's hooves, a still-vivid patch of red . . . she turned away.

There should be a dog's paw prints here too. But the wind was shifting snow into drifts, blurring the surface. It was impossible to spot Vinny's prints and follow a trail. She searched and searched, and all the time the tracks grew fainter, until she had to give up and accept that wherever Vinny had chosen to run, it was well away from here.

'Carly!' A voice called from the carpark. It was Cleo, standing there in her thin denim jacket, trying to pull her cuffs over her bare hands to keep them warm.

Carly ran to the wire fence.

'I just heard what happened. Do you know how he is?'

Carly shook her head, not trusting herself to speak.

'God, you must be freezing!' Cleo's teeth chattered, her straight black hair whipped across her face as the wind blew stronger still. 'Listen, I saw Vinny!'

'Where?' Carly ran to climb the broken fence. Finding the dog seemed the most important thing in the world right now. If – when – Hoody recovered, he would want to know that Vinny was safe.

'In the park at the back of your place!' Cleo was running with her, weaving between the cars parked by the supermarket, up the steps on to the railway footbridge. Their feet clattered along the wooden boards. 'About half an hour ago. He was by himself. At least I *think* it was Vinny!' She stopped at the pavement on City Road, faltering now.

Carly nodded. 'Thanks, Cleo.' She'd rather keep on looking by herself. 'Can you pass the word round for me? If anyone else feels like helping and they find Vinny, tell them to take him back to the Rescue Centre. We'll look after him until Hoody's better!'

If . . . if . . . if. The word hammered at her brain as she ran on into the park that backed on to her own street. It made sense that Vinny had been seen here – it was one of Hoody's favourite places for bringing him for walks. He would know the football hut and pitches, the criss-crossing paths, the pond with the rocky island in the middle. He would choose a place to shelter and wait for Hoody to come and find him.

But when Carly stopped to look around, the world that hit her was as strange and un-familiar as the surface of the moon. It was white and smooth. The skeletons of black trees groaned under branches laden with snow. The pond was iced over, leaving the ducks and geese stranded on the island. On a slope at the far end of the park, kids had gathered with red, yellow and blue sledges.

'Vinny!' She called and whistled. She went tramping across the snowy slopes. There were dogs here, but they were with owners, excited by the new landscape, ready to charge into drifts and bound out again in a flurry of wet fur and snow. She covered every corner, looking in vain for the mongrel's sturdy figure.

'Vinny!' Carly even tried calling across the frozen lake to the island in a last vain hope.

She waited, but she knew it was no good. A duck flew up from the rocks and circled overhead. A black-and-white collie came poking his nose into the frozen bushes at the water's edge. It was time to give up and go home.

4

Life was going on as normal at Beech Hill Rescue Centre. The lights were bright in reception, Bupinda was behind her desk, and Mel, their nurse, was busy carrying a litter of puppies from treatment room to kennels as morning surgery came to an end.

Carly recognised Geoff Best standing in the waiting room talking to her dad. A birdcage containing the noisy, moulting macaw was resting on a bench.

'*Eeaagh*!' Mac made his presence felt by shrieking and rattling his cage.

'You'll catch your death!' Mel tutted at her as she passed. 'You need a warm coat and scarf in this weather.'

Carly gave an empty smile. 'Is Steve back yet?'

'Haven't seen him. He rang. Something about having to wait at the hospital. I don't know what exactly.'

Obviously the news hadn't filtered through to Mel. As the warmth gradually worked its way into her body, Carly sighed. She could overhear the manager of the city farm arranging to give the abandoned macaw a home at Sedgewood.

'There's an ideal space for him just outside my office. It's nice and light, with a sloping glass roof and an indoor tree. We can construct an aviary for him, then Mac should be quite happy hopping about in there.'

'Tell visitors not to feed him crisps or sweets,' Paul Grey warned. 'And give him a chance to settle down first. He's been through a bad time by the look of things.'

Geoff promised to do his best. 'Thanks for thinking of us.' He shook hands and picked up the cage.

'*Eeee!*' Mac protested at being swung through the air.

'If he continues to pull out his feathers, give me a ring. I'll come and take another look.' Carly's dad followed the manager to the door. 'And listen, I know you've got money worries at the moment. Liz told me. So don't worry about our fees until things ease off, OK?'

Geoff gave him a grateful nod. Then, with Mac still shrieking and protesting, he went off.

Paul turned and spotted Carly. 'Upstairs!' He took one look and ordered her gently out of sight. With an arm around her shoulder he led her into the living room and eased her down on the sofa. 'Don't say anything, just stay there and get yourself warmed up.'

She flopped against the cushions. When her dad was this kind it made her want to cry.

He brought her hot sweet tea from the kitchen, a big sweater from her jumper drawer. 'No need to talk. Just drink this and listen.' He looked anxiously into her eyes. 'Steve's been keeping me up to date from the hospital. They're giving Hoody the very best care. He lost blood, but not too much, thanks to you.

He's badly bruised around his ribs and neck, and there's a lot of swelling, so they're waiting to X-ray him until tomorrow. Meanwhile, they're keeping him sedated.'

'Will he be able to walk?'

'We hope so. His sister's there with him.'

'Is he still asking for Vinny?' Silly question, she knew.

Paul nodded. 'And this Bones creature. He keeps telling Steve to go out and look for him.'

'Typical Hoody!' The donkey had half-killed him and he was still worried about him.

'Typical Carly!' her dad said softly, wiping away a tear from her cheek. 'I take it you've been looking?'

She nodded.

'No luck?' He didn't wait for an answer. Instead, he made a decision. 'Drink up and get that sweater on while I ring Steve and tell him we're going to meet him at the scene of the crime. The old railway yard, wasn't it?'

The hot sweet tea hit the back of her throat. She gulped and nodded again.

'Come on, no time to lose!' He wouldn't let her give in. Looking at his watch, he hauled her to her feet. 'I've got an hour and a half to spare before my next appointment with a Dobermann pinscher!'

It was snowing again when they met up with Steve, who had come over from St Mark's to Hillman's carpark as soon as Paul had phoned.

News from the hospital was still the same; Hoody was officially described as comfortable and Zoe was sitting patiently at his bedside.

'The kid's amazing,' Steve told them. 'Apparently he spent half of last night out here with the donkey in the freezing cold, trying to decide what to do.'

'That was my fault,' Carly admitted. She reminded her dad that she'd forgotten to turn up to give Hoody a hand. 'In fact, most of this is my fault. When you think about it, it could have been due to me that Bones went out of control. I was trying to show Hoody how to get him into the truck when it all went wrong.' For the first time she told them what was preying on her mind, shuddering as she recalled the thud of the donkey's hooves on the improvised ramp.

'You can't blame yourself,' Paul said. 'In fact, you were probably right; there was no point trying to force the donkey up the ramp. He would only respond to slow, careful handling. Hoody could never have dragged him in.'

'He didn't mean to be cruel. Maybe it looked like that, but Bones was wearing a head collar. The rope wasn't just looped round his neck!' She stuck up for her friend.

'Calm down, we're not saying it's anyone's fault.' Steve took his phone from his pocket as it began to ring. He looked suddenly intent, holding up his hand to warn them to be quiet as he listened to the message.

Carly waited, trying to shelter from the whirling snow by standing behind the van. Her heart sank again as she watched the wintry scene. *What animal could survive this*? she wondered.

'That was Bupinda,' Steve told them. 'She's just had someone else ring up to say he's spotted the donkey!'

'Whereabouts?' Paul Grey was ready for action.

'Not far from here. You know that building

site by the canal where they're renovating the old pub?'

'Victoria Wharf?' Carly's dad nodded and headed for his car. 'How long ago?'

'No more than five minutes. I'll bring the van and trailer. You and Carly go on ahead!'

They nodded and ran for the car. With a roar of the engine and squeal of skidding wheels, they were on their way.

Carly strapped herself in tight. Her father's car was fast and powerful, but the back streets were narrow. There were junctions and round-abouts, queues of cars at traffic lights. 'Can't we hurry up?' she pleaded.

So he cut down another side street, over a humped bridge across the canal. 'I think we can get to the Victoria this way,' he muttered. 'Now listen, when we get there, I don't want you rushing into things. By all accounts this animal is not only starving and freezing, he's also terrified. And a frightened donkey is unpredictable, remember. That makes him dangerous. Look what happened to Hoody.'

'So what do we do?' She felt her stomach

churn as the road suddenly dipped.

'Keep an eye on him. Wait for Steve to arrive with warm blankets and slings. I'll probably try to sedate him if I can get close enough.' He slowed down and turned into a street lined with high brick walls, blocked at the end by a screen of wooden boards sprayed with graffiti. There was a door cut into the screen that swung open.

'Is this it?' Carly asked.

'Through that little door. The old Victoria pub is behind there. It overlooks the canal.'

She opened the car door and ran across dirty, trampled snow. As the cold wind cut through her, she thought she heard yells and shouts from beyond the screen. It sounded like kids playing a rough game.

'Gotcha!' a boy's voice crowed.

'Look at him trying to run for it!'

'Go on, get him again!'

A snowball fight? A gang playing on the building site while the workmen took time off?

'Carly, hang on!' Paul Grey slammed the car door and shouted after her.

But she couldn't stop now. Bones was behind

there, probably terrified by whizzing snow-balls and the raucous yells.

'Watch it, I can hear someone coming!' a boy shouted.

As Carly reached the gate, a lump of hard snow thudded against the screen. She ducked just in time. Voices jeered.

'Missed!'

'Try again!'

'Never mind her, get the donkey!'

Carly swung her gaze round the scene. On the right was the old pub building with boarded windows. Sheets of blue plastic covered gaping holes in the roof, there were piles of snow-covered rubble against the door. Straight ahead was the wharf with a sudden drop into the frozen canal. And to the left a gang of boys and a fierce black dog stood on top of another mound of rubble.

She saw what they were aiming at and gasped. It was Bones. The donkey had fallen to his knees at the edge of the wharf, hardly able to hold up his head. His shaggy winter coat was matted with lumps of frozen snow as he tried in vain to lift himself and run away from the boys' cruel taunts.

'Stop it!' Carly slipped and struggled for balance as she set off across the building site to save Bones. 'Look what you're doing to him!'

Snowballs whizzed through the air towards her. Then one of the boys scooped up more snow, formed it into a rough ball and showed it to the dog. 'Fetch, Toby!'

The dog yelped and snapped. As the boy launched the snowball towards Bones, he leaped after it, bounding to catch it before it landed and smashed to pieces.

'Look at him go!' the boy laughed as the excited dog cannoned into the struggling donkey. His aim had been good.

Bones brayed feebly. He swung his head at the dog, teeth gnashing. Toby hit him in the side, rolled and snarled back. Then he was up on his feet, worrying and charging at the stricken animal. Fangs bared, he snapped and bit.

'Stop him!' Carly cried again. She was running as fast as she could towards the scrap, while the four boys on the mound of rubble stood by laughing.

Bones was too weak to resist. His legs had collapsed under him. He couldn't defend himself. But still he tried, snapping back with his yellow teeth, his ears laid flat, gums bared.

'Call him off!' Carly screamed. The dog had bitten Bones on the shoulder. As the donkey tossed his head, the trailing blue rope attached to his head collar snaked over the edge of the wharf, out of sight. She lunged to catch it. But the ground was solid ice. She slipped and lost her balance, the snaking rope caught round her leg and pulled taut, edging Bones still nearer to the frozen drop.

It all happened in a flash. As the donkey slid, his legs caught the snarling dog, who rolled again and jumped clear. Carly felt herself skid to the very edge of the wharf. She heard her father shout her name and the sudden silence of the jeering boys.

Then there were footsteps running away as she grabbed hold of a metal post used in the old days for mooring the canal barges. She stopped herself from skidding off the end of the wharf just in time, but Bones was struggling on the end of the rope. His own weight carried him sliding and braying over the edge.

There was a crash and a crack. The sound of water gurgling to the frozen surface. Carly looked down the two-metre drop to splintered ice and the shape of Bones struggling in the black water. He sank out of sight.

'Hold on to that rope!' Paul Grey yelled.

Carly took the strain. The weight of the donkey almost dragged her arms out of their sockets, but she held fast, using the metal post as a way of steadying herself. Then her dad arrived and lent his own weight. Together they pulled.

Bones's head broke the surface. He took a gasp of air, flailing with his front legs, smashing more ice.

Then Steve arrived with the ropes and slings he'd planned to use to get the donkey into the trailer. Quickly he took in the scene: the panicking animal in the water, the strain on the worn rope that he grabbed in order to help Carly and Paul.

'You can let go now,' he told Carly. 'I want you to go as carefully as you can along that broad wooden beam.' He pointed to one arm of the lock mechanism that spanned the canal. 'Take this sling with you, and if you can get near enough, try to put it under the donkey's belly to support him. Then we might be able to drag him out.'

Listening carefully to the inspector's calm instructions, she nodded. The sling was made of nylon fabric attached to strong straps and ropes. She could see that it was possible to use the beam to creep near enough to Bones to slip it under him.

'But be quick, Carly,' her dad told her. 'He won't survive long in that water. It's below zero in there.'

So she went along the beam on all fours, closer and closer to the frightened creature. She had to lean out to catch hold of his head collar, felt him wrench his head away, then give in weakly as she tugged his whole body against the lockside. She slid one end of the sling under him and waited for the ropes to float to the surface on the far side. Then she grabbed these again. 'Done it!' she called.

'Good girl!' Steve checked with Paul that he

could take the donkey's full weight with the frayed blue rope. Then he came to help Carly. 'We're going to edge him back to the wharf. Ready?'

She nodded. Holding on to the sling, they crept back along the beam. Bones struggled as he felt himself towed along.

'Steady!' Paul watched as Steve and Carly fought to keep their balance.

They paused and waited for Bones to stop tugging. He grew weaker by the second as the cold seeped through him. Then they began again, towing him until they reached firm ground and could look down on the donkey fast against the side of the wharf where he had first fallen in.

'OK, now we all need to heave as hard as we can.' Steve gave the final instruction. 'He's going to be heavy with all this water bogging him down, but I think the three of us should be able to do it!'

Paul came and they all took the strain. The nylon sling tightened under Bones's belly. They felt him lift in the water. Then they heaved again. He was clear, his legs trailing on the ice.

Carly felt as if her muscles would snap. The donkey seemed to weigh a ton. They were dragging him through the air, on to the wharf, water was running off his back, down his flanks, then he was on his side, ribs heaving, head tossing and twisting, lying alongside them.

'Let go!' Steve gasped.

The three of them collapsed forward to catch their breath.

'Blankets, Carly!' Once the donkey was on dry land, Paul took over.

She half-ran, half-scrambled to fetch them from the pile of rubble where Steve had dropped them. Then she staggered back and spread them over the shivering animal.

'OK, we need to prop his head up with something!'

She looked round, fetched some bricks, and while Steve gently held Bones's head clear of the ground, she shoved them underneath and padded them with a blanket to make a pillow. She watched her dad take a stethoscope and listen.

'Faint heartbeat,' he told them. 'We need to

fix him up with a drip here, then stretcher him back to the van.' He ran to his car to fetch the equipment he would need.

Carly rubbed the donkey warm while they waited. She stroked his neck, saw his eyes glazing over. 'It's OK now,' she promised. 'Everything's going to be all right!' *He must not go to sleep*! she told herself.

'Glucose solution,' Paul Grey explained, once he'd come running back. He inserted a needle attached to a sachet of clear liquid. 'To treat his malnutrition. He's got no body fat whatsoever; you can see every bone in his body. So he's got no insulation against the cold. We have to restore his body temperature and give him some fluid.'

'What about pneumonia?' Steve asked, resting back on his heels, watching anxiously.

'His lungs sound pretty bad,' Paul admitted. 'And there are these sores on his face. There's an infection there.' He checked the fresh dog bite on the shoulder. 'I'll give him a tetanus shot, then we'll lift him into the trailer, get him back to Beech Hill as quickly as we can.'

'There!' Carly told the donkey. She battled

with all her willpower to keep him awake. 'You don't give in, you hear!'

The donkey looked up at her as the two men lifted him quickly on to the stretcher. He seemed to respond to the sound of her voice.

She took the drip and carried it. 'You listen to me!' she insisted, talking all the time they crossed the building site and took him through the narrow door out into the street. 'We haven't gone through all this for nothing!'

Steve and Paul slid the stretcher on to the floor of the straw-lined trailer. They were going to lift the ramp and bolt it into position so they could drive off, but Carly insisted on climbing in beside Bones. 'I'll ride with you,' she promised. 'I'll make sure you keep your eyes open until we get you to the Rescue Centre.'

Her dad nodded and bolted them both in. 'Hold tight,' he warned.

Steve started the van, the trailer lurched forward. Beneath the blankets in the dark trailer the donkey lay quiet.

'Stay awake!' Carly insisted, praying that Bones was still listening. She saw his eyes glisten. 'Good boy!'

Willpower, staying conscious, not giving in. The trailer swayed out on to the main road, into the roar of traffic. Bones sighed and watched her every move.

Softly she reached out to stroke his face. 'What will I tell Hoody if you die on us now?' she pleaded gently.

5

They made a space for Bones in the large laundry room at Beech Hill.

It was midday on Saturday when they carried him in, too weak to stand, covered in sores and bites. Paul and Mel cleared the space, then lined the floor with straw. They lay the donkey down in a quiet corner and agreed to let Carly stay by his side.

Liz stood in the doorway shaking her head at the sight. 'It might be more humane not to treat him,' she told them. 'I've seen plenty of mistreated farm animals in my time, but hardly ever one as bad as this.'

'You don't rate his chances?' Paul asked quietly.

'I think we have to consider putting him to sleep.' It was hard to say, but she had to be honest. 'He's probably been wandering around looking for food for weeks,' she judged. 'Picking up what little he could from bins and tips. If he had an owner, the person made no attempt to keep him fed. Then when he was too weak to cope, I suppose they just dumped him by the railway line.'

'And left him to starve!' Carly's blood boiled. She would never, ever get used to some people's cruelty towards animals.

As she stroked Bones and he looked up at her with big, dark, almond-shaped eyes, she pleaded for them to help him. 'I know he's very weak, but if we start to feed him he'll gradually get his strength back!' Her brown eyes flashed; she wasn't going to give up on Bones even if everyone else did.

'Carly, it's not that simple.' Her dad crouched beside her. 'Bones is in a lot of pain. He's suffering from malnutrition, anaemia, infected wounds and possible pneumonia. His whole body's crawling with lice and fleas. The question is, would it be kinder to put him out of his misery?'

They all gazed at the shivering bundle lying under blankets on the bed of straw.

No! Carly told herself. 'All of that stuff can be treated!' she insisted.

Paul agreed that it could. 'He's already had a tetanus jab, but he'd need antibiotics, vitamin tablets, then de-worming and de-lousing. His hooves would have to be trimmed to help him to walk properly. Then there's all the nursing care.' He looked up at Liz to see if he'd missed anything.

'We'd have to X-ray him for broken bones after all the mistreatment he's been through. And we'd have to feed him very gradually, build him up slowly. It could take weeks.'

There was a long pause.

'Then there's another problem,' Steve added. 'We've made an emergency space for him here, but it's only temporary. Where would you put him if he needed long-term nursing care?'

'You could find a donkey sanctuary for him

to go to.' Carly had heard of special homes for unwanted donkeys out in the country.

'He wouldn't cope with a long journey,' Liz warned. 'If we did decide to try to save him, he mustn't be moved far.'

Carly understood. The problems twisted her in knots as she tried to see a way through. 'I wouldn't mind giving up my spare time to nurse him,' she offered.

Paul smiled. 'I know you wouldn't.' He turned to the others. 'What do you think?'

Bones's future hung in the balance. He'd survived weeks of cold and hunger, the cruelty of being tethered and dumped on city waste-land in snow by the most brutal of owners . . . Carly closed her eyes and waited for the decision.

'Let's try!' Liz said at last, rushing to fetch the antibiotics to begin work on saving the donkey's life.

'Vinny's vanished into thin air.' Cleo and Hanna came to the Rescue Centre later that afternoon. 'We've got kids looking everywhere for him.'

'Does Hoody know?' Carly had been so busy with Bones that she hadn't been able to ring the hospital.

'We don't think so.' Cleo bit her bottom lip. She was a small, usually bubbly girl with big brown eyes in a silky dark complexion. But now she looked deadly serious. 'In fact, we told his sister that Vinny was safe and sound here at Beech Hill. She probably passed on the message.'

'But he isn't!' Carly sat down on a bench in the waiting room, under photographs of dogs and cats that had been rescued. The lie sent her hot and cold all over.

'We know that.' Hanna looked embarrassed. She pushed her blonde hair behind her ears and sat down beside Carly. 'We didn't want to worry Hoody, that was all.'

'How can a dog just vanish?' Cleo wanted to know. 'It isn't like Vinny doesn't know his way around. He and Hoody are always out together.'

'*Were*,' Hanna reminded her. '*Were* always out together. Hoody for one's not going anywhere!'

'How is he?' To Carly it felt like days since the accident had happened. Yet it was only earlier that morning.

Cleo shrugged. ' "Comfortable". Whatever that means.'

'They're saying he's gonna be paralysed,' Hanna put in, her grey eyes wide and scared.

'*Who* says?' Carly cut her dead before the gossip could get into full swing. She stared back defiantly.

'OK, OK, don't bite my head off.' Hanna glanced round as Steve Winter came through the main door. 'So, do you want us to carry on looking for Vinny, or not?'

Carly sighed. 'Sorry. Yeah, that would be good.' She wracked her tired brains to think where else they could look. 'Have you tried Morningside?'

This was the tower block estate behind the park. Cleo nodded. 'He wasn't there. And we tried the whole of Beacon Street, yelling "Vinny!" at the top of our voices, in case he'd got trapped in an outside loo or something by mistake. No good.'

'Some of the other kids tried the King

Edward's Road allotments. They said there were a few dogs roaming around, but not Vinny.'

'Were they sure?'

'Pretty sure. Vinny comes when he's called, and they said all the dogs just ran off when they shouted.'

'It must be that pack of semi-wild ones,' Steve suggested. 'There's a whole gang of them roaming the streets at the moment. I bring a few in here and put them in the kennels, ready for adoption, whenever I get the chance.' He'd stopped to pin new posters on the notice-board. 'How's Bones?' he asked Carly, as Cleo and Hanna got ready to leave.

'Still on the drip.' She'd just left his side for the first time to come and talk to her friends. 'He's sleeping at the moment. Liz says the antibiotics might begin to work in another couple of hours. We have to keep our fingers crossed.'

'In that case, have you got time to come out on a job with me?' he asked. He held the door open for the girls.

'I'm not sure.' Carly hesitated. She didn't

know if she could bear to leave Bones. 'He might wake up while I'm out.'

'Yes, and we'll be here to look after him!' Liz popped her head out of a treatment room. 'Go on, Carly, it'll do you good, take your mind off things.' She promised to look in on the donkey every ten minutes to check his progress. 'He'll still be here when you come back, don't worry!'

So Carly gave in, said goodbye to Cleo and Hanna, and went in the van with Steve to see Bill Brookes at his pet shop on City Road. Steve explained the job as they drove.

'Bill wants to talk to us at the shop. He's got a few suspicions about this trade in exotic birds. I rang round all the city pet shops warning them not to buy from people selling parrots without the proper paperwork. It seems someone might have been in to Pampered Pets trying to offload some illegal macaws.'

'Like Mac?' she asked. The van swished through dirty pools of melting snow, and she noticed that the flakes had turned to a full, rainy drizzle.

He nodded as he pulled off the dual carriageway into a parking space in front of a row of shops. Bill Brookes's bright green door was open, and the owner was waiting for them as they arrived.

He was a thin man of about forty, with round, rimless glasses and wispy fair hair. Proud of his shop, he kept the animals clean and groomed and in good condition, so Carly liked him and the visits she made with Steve. The moment she stepped inside and breathed the smells of dog biscuits and sawdust, saw the antics of the hamsters in their cages, the silent gliding of blue, orange and gold fish in their heated tanks, she felt at ease.

'Glad you could come,' Bill said, rapid-fire as always. His words rattled out like bullets. 'I've been thinking about what you said on the phone, Steve, and I've put two and two together!'

'You think you know something about these macaws?' The inspector took off his gloves and laid them on the counter.

'Listen to this! A bloke comes in last week with a couple of parrots and a blue and gold macaw. Tries to sell them to me, but I wasn't having any. Like you say, I have to see the paperwork before I buy anything from him, and he made some excuse about it being held up in the post.'

'What did he look like?'

'Baldish, fattish, wearing a leather jacket.'

'And a big gold watch?' Carly asked.

Bill raised his eyebrows and nodded.

'Did he sniff a lot?'

'How did you know?'

'It's the same man who brought Mac into the surgery,' Carly told them. 'But he told us that he'd bought Mac off someone else, that he'd only had him for a week.'

'Looks like he was being economical with the truth,' Steve grinned. 'In other words, he was lying. He's probably the one who's been importing these birds illegally.'

'It's worth a lot of money,' Bill explained. 'I can sell a macaw for several hundred pounds, and a parrot for not much less.'

Carly gasped. 'I feel sorry for them in any case, being kept in tiny cages. They belong in the jungle.'

'Not if they've been bred in captivity,' Steve reminded her. 'That's what happens; the eggs are hatched by breeders in South America, say, and when the young ones are old enough, they're put into crates and shipped to Europe. Often they arrive in terrible condition.'

'Some don't last the journey,' Bill added. 'Steve would tell you that.'

'It's true. They're crammed in without proper food or water. Sometimes I'm called in by the customs officials at the airport. When we open the crates, we find dead birds mixed in with the living ones, and the whole crate is filthy. But we're lucky if we can issue a summons and get the person responsible to court. Usually the address on the crate just leads us to an empty office or a derelict workshop and we can't lay our hands on the culprits back in South America either. It's a real problem.'

'So that's why this bloke's visit last week set me thinking. He left me a phone number in case I changed my mind.' Bill held up a scrap of paper with the number written on. 'I just rang him to say I had!'

'Well done! What did he say?' Steve asked eagerly. He winked at Carly.

'He said he'd be over in five minutes.' The pet shop owner went back to the door. 'In fact, this could be him now!'

A black car drew up alongside the Rescue Centre van and the man who'd brought Mac to Beech Hill got out. Carly recognised him straight away, watching through the shop window as he opened the back of the car and lifted out a square plastic pet carrier. 'Uh-oh!' She saw him pause as he registered the name on the side of their van. 'We should have parked out of sight.'

Steve clicked his tongue. He didn't want the man to change his mind now. 'Let's go!' he decided, leading the way out of the shop, followed by Bill and Carly.

The second the man saw Steve's uniform, he slid the box back into the car and slammed the door. He was racing for the driver's seat, fitting his key into the ignition, when Steve grabbed the door and held his arm. From the back of the car, the birds set up a loud screeching.

'Oh no, you don't!' Steve managed to wrest the key from the lock. 'I take it you've got proper export permits for these birds?'

'Who says I need them?' The man sat sullenly in his seat. He stared straight ahead.

'The law does, that's who.' Steve held on to the key and told Bill and Carly to open the boot of the car. 'And I need quarantine certificates and all the other necessary papers to prove you're the legal owner.'

'You'll be lucky!' the man sneered. There was no point lying or trying to pretend.

As Carly took one end of the box, the birds inside squawked and pecked at the wire front. She kept her fingers well clear of their hooked beaks, glimpsed a beautiful macaw with a gold body, blue wings and vivid black markings around his eyes.

'Failing that, I have to issue you with this summons to appear in court,' Steve went on.

The man carried on glowering straight ahead, biting the edge of his thumb, refusing to answer as Steve thrust a paper into his other hand. Then Steve took the vehicle registration number so that he could check the name of the owner on the police computer. It was the surest way of bringing the man to court.

'What do you want us to do with the birds?'

Carly asked. There seemed to be two others besides the macaw, one white, one mostly green.

'No proof of ownership, so we take them away,' Steve decided. He gave up on trying to get any information out of the man. 'One thing's for sure, I bet we can find better homes for them than the one they've been used to!' He let go of the car door and the man slammed it shut.

'Poor things!' Carly agreed. As she and Bill carried them to the van and the culprit drove off, she felt pleased that the rescue of the birds had gone smoothly. 'What about Mr Best at Sedgewood? Do you think he'd take care of them for us?' she asked Steve as he joined them.

'To keep Mac company, you mean?' He considered the option. 'It would certainly be a big new attraction for visitors, and it sounds as if the farm could do with it.'

'If they've got room. But, if they've got to build a new aviary for Mac, they might as well keep other birds in it too!' To Carly it seemed a brilliant solution, coming as it did at the end of a bad day.

'Do you want me to give him a ring for you?' Bill offered. New customers were going into the shop, so he set off to follow them inside.

'No, it's not far. We'll call in with three unexpected guests!' Steve decided it was best to go in person.

He too was in a good mood. He checked that the cage was secure in the back of the van, putting both hands over his ears as the birds set up a screeching protest. He urged Carly into the front seat. 'Come on, Carly, get your earplugs out!'

She grinned back and fastened her seat belt, realising they were in for a noisy ride!

6

'He got through the night.' Carly sat nervously by the side of Hoody's hospital bed, telling him the latest news about Bones. 'I sat up with him till midnight, until we were sure that the antibiotics were staring to work.'

Hoody lay flat, his neck held rigid by a plastic collar. There were dark purple bruises on his forehead and cheekbone. He didn't reply.

'Can he hear me?' she asked Zoe.

'Course he can!' Hoody's sister frowned. 'You haven't gone deaf, have you, Jon?'

'I heard.' He kept his eyes fixed on the white ceiling. 'What did he need antibiotics for?' he asked reluctantly.

'Pneumonia.' She'd told him the story of the fall into the canal, listed all the things that were still wrong with Bones. 'But his temperature's coming down now. Liz says that's because the medicine's taking effect. And he ate some hay early this morning.'

'Does that mean he's gonna be OK?'

'We hope so. Dad says we can take X-rays later today. Sunday's supposed to be our quiet day, so there'll be time to do that later on. And we're trying to decide what to do with him when he's strong enough to be moved. We can't keep him in the laundry room at Beech Hill for very long!' She forced herself to sound more cheerful than she felt. Really, the sight of Hoody lying flat on his back, his pale face bruised, eyes staring at the ceiling, had shocked her more than she could show.

'You hear that, Jon?' Zoe did her best to cheer him up. 'You feel happy now?' When there was no answer, she looked across the bed at Carly. 'You should've heard him before you came and gave him the good news. It was "Bones this" and "Bones that"! I couldn't stop him fretting about the blooming animal!'

'I knew you'd want to know what had happened,' Carly said softly. She hoped that hearing Bones was safe would help Hoody to get better himself. Her dad had driven her over to the hospital specially to tell him. 'He means a lot to you, doesn't he?'

Hoody's eyes flickered.

'Me too,' she confessed. 'You know the amazing thing? You'd think Bones would be really vicious after everything that's been done to him, wouldn't you? Well, he isn't. Now that he trusts us, he's as friendly and gentle as anything!' She described how the donkey now had enough strength to lift his head at the sound of their voices in the corridor, how he nuzzled his soft nose against her hand when she sat beside him.

'You'll be able to see that for yourself soon,' Zoe assured Hoody. 'When they let you out of here!'

He turned his eyes away and stared at the wall.

SKIN AND BONE

Then nurses came to take his temperature and check his position. They told Zoe that there was a chance he would be going for X-ray early the next morning. Hoody endured it all in silence, but as soon as one of the nurses drew his sister away from the bed to give her more information, he spoke to Carly.

'How's Vinny?' he asked in his cold, clear voice.

She took a sharp breath. She thought she'd prepared herself for the inevitable question, but there was just too much hesitation for her to lie easily. 'OK,' she said faintly.

'How is he?' he said again.

It was like a knife being turned in her insides.

'You don't know, do you?' he said slowly, accusingly. His eyes swivelled towards her to study her face. 'Why not? They told me he'd run back to Beech Hill.'

'They didn't want to worry you.' She felt herself blush to the roots of her dark hair.

'But he didn't, did he?'

Carly shook her head.

'What happened to him?'

'We don't know.' Her voice was a whisper. She had to steel herself to tell him the truth. 'He's still missing. But everyone's out looking for him. He's bound to turn up eventually!'

Instead of swearing and making a fuss, Hoody just turned his eyes away.

'Oh, I'm sorry!' She felt dreadful, imagining how it must feel to be lying helpless in a hospital bed.

'It's OK. I knew, anyway.' He sounded flat, empty.

'How?'

'I just did. He wouldn't go back to Beech Hill, would he? It was a stupid lie. He'd go to Beacon Street. That's Vinny; I know him. If he'd been OK he'd have gone straight home to look for me!'

What should have been a quiet day at Beech Hill turned busy with emergencies. The bad weather meant more minor traffic accidents, and it was often the bad luck of a family pet to get in the way of skidding cars. So while Liz was dealing in the prep room with a black-and-white cat with a broken pelvis, Paul took on a twelve-week-old puppy rushed to the centre with a serious viral infection. The owner told him that the little brown spaniel cross had been vomiting for twenty-four hours.

Carly watched her dad examine the puppy's mouth and throat. He took the dog's temperature and showed her how to do a dehydration test by gently pinching the loose skin at the scruff of the patient's neck. 'If the skin doesn't return to its normal position, it means the animal is seriously dehydrated,' he explained.

'It's serious, then?' The elderly female owner was worried.

'I take it she hasn't any appetite?'

'No.'

'And she's been listless like this for quite a while?' The puppy had sunk its head on to its front paws and lay still.

'Yes. What's she got, doctor?' The old lady sounded confused. Her face crumpled and her mouth twitched as she looked down at the little dog.

'Well, it's not distemper, but it could be the parvo virus. We'll have to keep her in and give her fluid through a drip, plus a course of antibiotics.'

'And will that do the trick?'

'We hope so. But the treatment isn't cheap. Do you need a few minutes to decide what to do?'

'Will she die without it?'

Paul nodded. 'Even if we start treatment now, we can't guarantee a result.' He waited for a decision.

'I want you to go ahead,' the old lady said with a nod. 'I don't care what it costs.'

'Are you sure?'

She nodded again, so Paul told Carly to take the puppy into the isolation unit upstairs.

'What's her name?' she asked, letting the owner stroke her pup and say goodbye.

'Rosie.' There were tears in the old lady's eyes.

So Carly took Rosie up to Mel, who attached her to a drip and put her into a heated intensive care unit. Then she went downstairs to call in on Bones.

The donkey was now able to sit, head up, taking notice of his surroundings. He was off his glucose solution drip, taking water by mouth. Carly took a handful of hay from a net bag hanging on the laundry room door and offered it to him. He nibbled daintily, chomping and grinding with his big yellow teeth.

Carly stroked his white muzzle and pushed his shaggy mane from his eyes. She could see that the sores on his face and shoulder were already beginning to heal.

'Slow but sure,' Liz said as she looked in on them. 'He's certainly looking better, isn't he?'

Carly nodded. 'Thanks for agreeing to give him a chance.' Bones nuzzled her hand again, demanding attention.

'But he's not out of the woods yet, you know.' Liz didn't want her to get the wrong impression. 'We can't be sure that his heart and other organs haven't been affected. And there's still the problem with his lungs.' She came in and took her stethoscope out of her pocket. She pressed it against the donkey's side. 'Take a listen to this.'

Carly fixed the stethoscope into her ears and leaned forward.

'Can you hear that rough, rasping sound?

That's fluid inside the tiny air sacs in the lung. Luckily it's only on one side at the moment, but if it spreads to the other lung and becomes double pneumonia, then we're really in trouble.'

The noise upset Carly. It reminded her how sick Bones was. She wanted somehow to push it to the back of her mind, so she began to tell Liz about her successful visit to Sedgewood with Steve the night before. 'We didn't know if Geoff Best would want to take the birds, but he took one look at them and said yes!'

'That was lucky. I suppose he thinks the macaws will be nice for the children who visit the farm.'

'And company for Mac. They've already started work on building an indoor aviary next to the office. We saw a couple of volunteers helping Geoff with the carpentry work.'

Liz took Bones's temperature while she was listening and noted the result on his chart. 'Good. How was George's cracked heel?'

'Better. But Geoff says he'll have to go back to the brewery soon because they can't afford the feed bills at the farm.'

'That's a pity.' Satisfied for now with how Bones was progressing, she stood up, hands in the pockets of her white coat. 'I had been thinking that Sedgewood might offer us a place for this fellow as soon as he's well enough to be moved.' The problem of what to do with Bones long term loomed large in everyone's minds.

'That would be great,' Carly said wistfully. 'You hear that, Bones? There's a city farm near here that would be a perfect home for you.'

'Except that they haven't any money,' Liz reminded her. 'I've even heard on the grapevine that they might be forced to close next year. Something about losing part of their grant from the city council.'

Carly sighed. 'Why isn't anything ever simple?' If Bones did get better, Sedgewood was about the best place he could be. He'd have a nice warm stable in the winter and green fields to graze on in the spring. Visitors would stream in to see him and make a fuss of him. He need never be hungry or lonely again.

'Because . . .' Liz shrugged, 'because life isn't simple.' She gave Carly a sympathetic smile

before she went off to X-ray the injured cat.
'Anyway, let's take one step at a time. We have
to get Bones back on his feet before we map
out his whole future for him!'

'Have you heard the latest on Hoody?'
    'He's got some kind of swelling on his brain.
He can't move!'
    'What, never?'
    'They're not saying. But everyone reckons
he's paralysed! He'll have to go round in a
wheelchair!'
    From the second Carly walked into school next
morning, the whole talk was about the accident.
Carly heard the rumours in every corridor and
every classroom and denied them all.
    'How do you know it's not true?' Hoody's
mates swarmed round her.
    'She was there, wasn't she, stupid?' Cleo
stepped in and shoved them back. 'Tell them
what happened, Carly.'
    She told the story a dozen times. Yes, the
donkey had reared up and landed on Hoody.
Yes, he was unconscious and there was blood.
    'What did you do? Who called the

ambulance? How long did you have to wait?'
They wanted every last detail.

'What about Vinny?' she asked in return.
'Has anyone got any idea what's happened to
him?'

They all shrugged and shook their heads.

'Maybe someone found him, thought he was
a stray and went off with him. He probably
got a new home by now.'

'Or he got lost and he's living rough.'

'Maybe he ran under the wheels of a car. He
could be lying dead in a ditch.'

The rumours grew wilder until Mr Howell
walked into the room and called the register.
He was stony-faced as he made the official
announcement about Hoody's accident.

'Now you've all no doubt heard what happened to Jon Hood on Saturday morning. The
news from the hospital is that he's in a stable
condition, but I don't want you all to go
rushing over to St Mark's to visit him. His sister
has been in touch with the school to say that
they want family visitors only. So I thought the
tutor group could get together and write letters
instead.'

There was an uneasy silence. What kind of letter did you write to someone who might be paralysed for the rest of his life? Carly felt herself go hot then cold. She sensed all eyes were on her and blaming her for what had happened.

Mr Howell sat at his desk surveying the group. 'This is a difficult time,' he admitted. 'But we just have to wait for test results and hope that Hoody's injuries aren't as serious as we fear.'

The use of the nickname made everyone stare. It suddenly made the teacher seem more human. He cleared his throat. 'Meanwhile, I've got an important notice to read out. It's about the charity fund-raising week we held before Christmas. Now I'm pleased to say the school raised more money than ever before, thanks to your efforts.'

Carly let her attention drift as Mr Howell congratulated them and told them the total amount. She couldn't get the picture of Hoody lying in his hospital bed out of her mind.

'. . . As you know, part of the money is to go to a national charity that's already been decided on. But the rest of the money raised is to be given to a local charity, and this is what I want you to think about today. It means we'll be giving money to a good cause here in the city, to benefit local people.' He explained clearly so that they understood the difference. 'This is a lot of money, and we have to think carefully. So talk about it amongst yourselves, decide which good cause you'd like to support. And if anyone has a suggestion, I'd like to hear it by the end of the week.'

'Sir!' A boy on the back row stuck up his hand. 'Let's give it all to Hoody, sir!'

There was a murmur of approval. But the teacher shook his head. 'Hoody deserves all your kind thoughts, Darren, but he isn't a charity. You need to think of something that's run to help others, or that offers something special to the community. Take your time. I'm sure you'll find exactly the right thing.'

But Carly didn't need time. She'd tuned back in when Darren had put up his hand. She'd heard the words 'charity... help others ... community' and knew the answer in a flash.

Her hand shot up, all eyes were back on her

as she blushed deep red and stammered out her suggestion. They would say she had a one-track mind, they would think of all the reasons not to agree with her, but she went ahead anyway. 'I think we should give it to Sedgewood City Farm,' she said.

7

'How's Bones?' Hoody asked Carly. He was still strapped into the plastic collar, lying flat on his back.

It was Monday tea-time when she'd taken the phone call from Zoe Hood, asking her to come to the hospital. 'He's been nagging me to see you,' she'd explained, 'I know we said family visitors only, but Hoody can't get these two animals out of his head. It's "Bones . . . Bones . . . Bones, Vinny . . . Vinny . . . Vinny!" And you're the only one who can give him the answers.'

So Carly had left Beech Hill and come into the city to St Mark's. Zoe had met her in the corridor, on her way to the cafeteria. The progress report on Hoody was only so-so, she'd said. They'd managed to do X-rays and found pressure from fluid inside his skull. It could be dangerous. They were hoping it would drain away naturally; if not, they would have to do an operation. 'He's been told he can't move. It's driving him mad not being able to sit up,' she'd confided. 'See if you can cheer him up for us!'

The news about Bones was pretty good. 'He's still off the drip, eating and drinking OK. Liz has given him the treatments for lice and fleas. The antibiotics have helped the sores and the bite to heal. Now there's just the pneumonia.' She ticked things off on her fingers. 'Provided he's strong enough to fight it, that should clear up in a day or two.'

Hoody listened intently, his eyes fixed on Carly's face. His bruised cheek had gone puffy and swollen, but the rest of his face was a ghastly white. His dark eyes bored into her.

She tried to hold his gaze, to convince him

that everything in the outside world was going fine. But she couldn't. She dropped her eyes to the bedspread and began to fiddle with one corner.

'That was the good news, wasn't it?' he muttered.

She nodded.

'So what's the bad?'

'Vinny still hasn't shown up. We're looking everywhere. But we haven't *heard* anything bad, so that could be a good thing in a way!' She twisted the corner of the white bedspread into a small peak. 'You know, like, if anything terrible had happened to him, someone would have let us know by now.'

Carly trailed off. Even to herself she didn't sound convincing.

'You mean, no news is good news?' Hoody was scornful.

'Something like that. Listen, Vinny can take care of himself. Cleo said she saw him in the park after you'd had your accident. That means he didn't run off and get knocked over by a car. He was still alive!'

'So where is he?'

'Not far. We'll find him.' She could be stubborn too. 'Anyway, your sister said I had to cheer you up, so do you want some more good news?' She smoothed the bedspread and moved her chair in closer.

'If you like.' Poor Hoody couldn't even give his usual shrug.

'There's this idea we've got at school of what to do with all the money we raised for charity before Christmas, remember? Some of us want to give it to Sedgewood . . .'

'What's that when it's at home?' He made himself sound deliberately bored.

'The city farm. And before you drift off to sleep, there's something you might want to know!' If he hadn't been so ill, she could have had an argument with him now. Sometimes he was so maddening. He opened his eyes to stare at the ceiling. 'Sedgewood really needs the money. Howler thought it was a great idea, so he says he'll put Sedgewood's name on the list with the suggestions from other tutor groups. On Wednesday the whole school gets to vote!'

Hoody sighed. 'Yeah, great.'

'Listen, this is important, if you only realised! The charity donation would help the farm to stay open. It's really short of money at the moment. It can't even pay our vets' bills! And . . .' Carly paused to give her announcement a big impact.

'And?' Even Hoody had to admit he was interested. He fixed his eyes on her again.

'We've had this idea . . .'

'Who's we?'

'Liz and me. You know what would be really great for Bones when he gets better?' There, Hoody was interested now. Carly couldn't hide a grin of triumph. 'If he could go and live at Sedgewood, in a proper stable, with loads to eat!'

'Fields to run around in?' Hoody asked.

'No work!'

'No lousy owner?'

'Loads of visitors to make a fuss of him. And we'd be able to visit. What do you say?'

He thought about it. Slowly a grin spread from ear to ear. 'This city farm, what other animals has it got?' he asked, the colour flooding back into his face.

* * *

Rosie the spaniel cross was fighting the virus that had made her so sick. She took water through a dropper, her temperature slowly going down.

'Carly, your dad needs a hand in Room 1,' Mel told her as she took a new patient into the cattery. 'As soon as you've finished with Rosie there.'

Evening surgery was coming to an end. There would be tables to clean down with disinfectant, the dogs in the kennels to feed and exercise. Though Carly didn't show it, she was tired after her visit to the hospital.

But she patted and stroked the young dog and left her snug in the isolation unit. In the treatment room she found that her father needed her help to untangle the fur of a neglected long-haired silver tabby cat. She set to with a steel comb, knowing that if she failed to get through the matted coat, the glorious fur would have to be shaved off. So she concentrated hard, parting the hair into sections and working on one small area at a time.

It was eight o'clock and Carly was still hard at work when Liz came through from next door. 'I was just going to take a look at Bones,' she told her. 'Thought you might like to come with me.'

'As soon as I've finished here.' The silver tabby was staying overnight, ready for her owner to come and collect her in the morning. So, with her coat newly soft and silky, Carly took her upstairs. She would go and see Bones, then ring round her friends to see if there was any news of Vinny. *Three days missing in the coldest part of the year. But Vinny was tough, he'd survived this kind of thing before.* Carly's thoughts went round in circles as she came downstairs.

The first sign of something wrong was her dad coming out of the flat, too worried to notice her. He took the stairs into the empty reception two at a time, and vanished down the corridor leading to the laundry room.

Something clicked in her head. She hurried after him.

'You see this?' Liz was pointing to Bones's mouth, to a trickle of saliva. The donkey sat quietly in his makeshift stall, his lower lip drooping. He seemed to be breathing quickly and lolling his head from side to side.

Paul Grey nodded. He moved in to take the patient's pulse. 'Too fast,' he noted, his eyes filled with concern.

'What is it? What's wrong with him?' Carly could see a change for the worse. Bones didn't even look at her as she came in. 'Has the pneumonia spread to the other lung?' She went and knelt beside the sick animal, putting her arms round his neck and resting his wobbly head against her chest.

'No, it's not that,' Liz said quietly. She turned to Paul. 'I thought it could be hyperlipaemia.'

He nodded again. 'Quite possibly. You see how he looks drunk?' Paul wanted to explain to Carly using words she would understand. 'This can happen with pneumonia in animals that come to us in very poor condition, like Bones here. He's so thin he's got no fat reserves. He's had next to no food for weeks, so the body has used up all its fat and what little that was left has moved straight to the liver, and from there it's got into the bloodstream, where it doesn't belong. It's affected his circulation. That's why he's breathing fast and his pulse rate is rapid. Liz spotted the main symptom, which is the dribbling from the mouth.' He waited to see if Carly understood. When she nodded, he went on.

'We call it hyperlipaemia. Liz is going to check the diagnosis by taking a blood sample. If the sample looks milky white, we'll know we're right.'

Carly held on to Bones as Liz took a syringe and extracted blood from a vein. He seemed to have recognised her and tried to rest his heavy head against her. He looked at her with his enormous dark eyes, as if to say, *What now*?

'It's OK,' she whispered. 'Everything's going to be fine!'

'We have to wait for it to settle.' Paul stood beside Liz under the fluorescent light in the warm atmosphere of the laundry room. Liz squirted the sample into a test tube, stoppered it and held it up to the light. Sure enough, the serum in the tube turned milky.

Liz sighed. 'As if pneumonia wasn't enough!'

Carly's father put his head to one side. 'This

is certainly going to set him back,' he agreed.

'So what do we do?' Carly felt helpless. She wished she knew as much about illnesses as her dad and Liz. Not knowing made her scared. She stroked Bones's neck and whispered words of comfort into his ear, but kindness alone wouldn't cure him of this new, dreadful relapse.

'We give him fluid – more glucose and this time bicarbonate,' Paul said briskly. 'Back on the drip, I'm afraid.'

'At home on the farm we used to find that a daily injection of insulin helped with horses who had hyperlipaemia,' Liz told him. 'It could make all the difference, even if we only caught it in the later stages.'

Paul agreed to give it a try. 'Don't worry,' he told Carly, 'we'll try everything we can.'

Liz crouched at Carly's side. 'But you have to realise it's even more serious now,' she said gently. 'Bones's liver could be badly damaged, as well as his heart.'

Biting her lip, swallowing hard, Carly nodded. She wouldn't let go of Bones until they'd finished putting needles in him and fixing up the drips. She stroked his soft fur, sensed him grow weary with all this treatment that didn't seem to make him any better, in spite of all the care lavished on him. He sank his head against her while the work went on. When Liz and Paul had finished and stood back, beckoning Carly to come with them and leave the patient to rest, he sighed and lay his head in the straw, looking up at her with a long suffering sigh.

'He's hanging on, isn't he?' Carly whispered, standing at the door before Liz turned off the light.

'By a thread,' Paul murmured. The room went dark and they closed the door. 'Now all we can do is wait.'

The long night passed. Carly fell asleep at midnight with Ruby curled at the end of her bed. She woke at six in the pitch dark, lay awake until seven, then slid out of bed without disturbing the cat. She went straight down to the surgery to check on Bones.

Her bare feet padded along the tiled corridor. She caught sight of her own reflection in the dark window – a slight figure in a white T-shirt belonging to her dad, with wavy dark hair and big, staring eyes. She listened for sounds from the laundry room, afraid that all she would hear would be silence.

There was a rustle in the straw, so she opened the door and let the light from the corridor filter in. Bones raised his head. He snickered softly.

So she crept inside, and spent half an hour at his side before her dad got up. She settled into the straw, talked to the donkey and stroked him, and was overjoyed when he responded. He nuzzled her hand, eased himself stiffly so that he could lean against her. For an animal who had been so abused, he was unbelievably friendly and loving back. Carly sighed, realising she must be only the second person in Bones's life who had shown him affection. The first had been Hoody, of course. She sighed again.

Then her dad came downstairs to look in on the patient. 'Better,' he said, after he'd checked the pulse and renewed the drips. 'The pulse rate is down at least. That's the first part of the crisis over. Now we have to stabilise him and get him back on to solid foods.' He looked at Carly's worried face. 'You haven't been here all night, have you?'

She shook her head. Soon it would be time to get ready for school, patients would be queuing for surgery, and the day would begin. Already there was the sound of the main door being unlocked from the outside.

'That'll be Steve,' Paul guessed. 'You go and see what brings him in so early while I finish off here.'

So she praised and patted Bones one last time and went through to reception to meet the inspector. He came in tramping fresh snow, his coat buttoned to the neck, with two dogs muzzled and leashed.

'No peace for the wicked,' he joked, switching on lights and handing one of the dogs to Carly.

'Where did these come from?' she asked. Both were mongrels, skinny as whippets, but with touches of all sorts in their pointed faces, floppy ears and bushy tails. One was mostly black with white paws and chest, one brown and fawn with black splodges on his back.

'I got a call at seven o'clock to go out to Morningside. Apparently there was an unholy row going on in a dustbin area at the back of one of the blocks of flats.' Steve took off his hat and shook it free of snow. 'I knew what it was straight away – this pack of half-wild strays we keep hearing about. So I seized the chance to go along and bring a couple in, since we have two free kennels at the moment. These were the first two I could lay my hands on. The others all ran off as soon as I drove up.'

Carly felt sorry for the thin, ownerless creatures. Neither had a collar and neither looked as if it had had a square meal for weeks. Here at Beech Hill they would have a full health check, be innoculated and chipped with an identity number, then put up for adoption. Any behaviour problems would be looked at by their visiting expert, Julie Sutton. Hopefully, some kind person would soon come along to the kennels, take a shine to them and take them home.

So they took the dogs into the kennels. The lights went on to a hearty barking and leaping up at the wire mesh doors. Up and down the rows, the residents greeted the new arrivals.

Carly was used to the noise and the activity. She said a word or two to each dog as she passed, found an empty kennel and led the black one in. She gave him water and waited for him to settle down, while Steve did the same for the other. Gradually the barking died down enough for them to hear themselves think.

'One thing I meant to mention,' Steve said with what Carly thought was a forced casual manner, as if he wasn't sure whether or not to say it. 'Now, I may be wrong, so don't take this as definite by any means.' He paused to wait for her in the corridor.

She closed the kennels door, trying not to get worked up. Steve was always calm and laid back, but even he had a glint of excitement in his eye. 'Tell me anyway,' she pleaded.

'OK. You know Hoody's missing dog?'

'Vinny.' The question was only another delaying tactic. Carly could hardly wait for Steve to spit it out. 'Yes, go on!'

'He's a brown stripy character with a streak of bulldog or boxer in him, isn't he?'

'Yes. You've seen him hundreds of times! So what?'

'Well, remember it was still dark, so I wouldn't go getting your hopes up too high.' He took the plunge. 'But I did have chance to get a pretty good look at them as they ran under a street light, and honestly, Carly, I think Vinny was a member of the pack that ran away!'

8

The word went round school. 'Vinny's alive! He's joined a gang of wild dogs! All we have to do is track them down, grab him and take him back to Beacon Street!'

'When?'

'Tonight.'

'Won't it be dark?'

'Yeah. So?'

'How will we find them?'

'Are you sure it's true?'

'How wild are these dogs, anyway?'

By lunch-time, everyone had the same story:

'Vinny's gone vicious. He's biting everything in sight. He's acting crazy, like he's got rabies!'

'That's stupid!' Carly stood in the dinner queue with Cleo and Hanna. It was the boys who picked up the worst rumours and believed them. 'We don't have rabies in this country!'

'Says you!' Darren Simpson wasn't keen on joining the search party after school that night. He was one of the ones who was spreading the rabies story in the first place, saying he lived on the Morningside estate and had seen and heard the dogs that morning. 'How do you know?'

Carly glanced round the dinner hall. 'If you don't believe me, ask Mr Howell. He's a biology teacher, isn't he?'

The boy backed down. 'OK, so it's not rabies. But no one in their right mind would go near that lot. They're dead vicious.'

Cleo stepped in on Carly's side. 'So we're just gonna forget about Vinny and walk away? What are we gonna tell Hoody when he gets out of hospital?'

'*If*,' Darren said gloomily. He believed all the

bad stories. 'Haven't you heard? He's got a brain tumour.'

Carly shook her head. 'It's not a tumour!'

'Oh, so you know everything?' He grew angry, mimicking her. ' "It's not rabies! It's not a tumour!" '

'Break it up, you two.' Mr Howell walked across at the sound of raised voices. He drew Carly to one side and spoke sympathetically. 'I wanted to tell you, I put in the bid to get the charity money donated to Sedgewood City Farm. Word in the staffroom is that it sounds like a pretty good idea. Other teachers are going to encourage their tutor groups to vote for it tomorrow.'

She put on a brave face and smiled. 'That's great, thanks.' Her mind was still on Darren Simpson. What if he went round telling the others not to risk going out to look for Vinny? Here she was, relying on getting as many people to join a search party as possible.

Mr Howell looked closely at her and mistook her worried look. 'Are you still anxious about Hoody?' he asked. 'Do you know how he is?'

Carly gave him the news from the night

before. The dinner queue shuffled forward, but now she didn't feel like eating. She stepped to one side to let Hanna and Cleo pass.

The teacher listened, then took an envelope out of his pocket. 'I'll tell you what,' he suggested. 'This is a get-well card for Hoody signed by all his teachers. Instead of me putting it in the post, why don't you miss the first lesson of afternoon school and take it to the hospital personally for us?' He waited for Carly to take it. 'Go on, I'm giving you official permission to skive!'

Giving another weak smile, she took the card. 'I'll go now, then.'

She left quickly, using the back way out of school before anyone could ask her what she was up to. She wanted to do the errand without any fuss; a quick bus ride there and back. With a bit of luck she would be able to hand the card over to Zoe without having to see Hoody; until she had definite good news about Vinny, she didn't fancy facing him again.

But it didn't go according to plan. *Nothing ever does*, she said to herself. As she approached the ward and passed Hoody's ground floor window, she glanced in and he saw her. Now there was nothing for it but to breeze in and give him the card personally. *Hi, how are you? . . . Flat on my back, stuck inside this plastic collar! How do you think?* Carly pushed through the sets of swing doors, rehearsing what she could say to cheer him up.

'Good news!' Zoe Hood intercepted her as she went up to the last set of doors. 'The doctors have taken another set of X-rays. They say the swelling inside his skull is going down by itself. Hoody won't need an operation!' Relief lit up her face as she dashed down the corridor to phone Dean.

'That's fantastic!' Carly heaved a sigh and went in with the card.

Hoody still couldn't turn his head because of the collar, but his eyes flicked in her direction. 'You haven't found Vinny, have you?' he demanded.

'Not yet.' She made a split-second decision not to tell him about the pack of dogs on the estate. She didn't want to raise his hopes. Slipping the card on to the bed, she tried to keep his mind on the doctors' news. 'Zoe just told me you won't need surgery. When are they going to let you out of this collar?'

'Dunno.' He refused to sound pleased.

'Soon, I expect.' In the silence that followed, she tried a different tack. 'Howler says we stand a good chance of getting the money for the farm.'

Hoody closed his eyes and sighed.

Carly rushed on. 'And Bones is doing OK. He had a sort of relapse last night, but you don't want to know the complications, do you? All that matters is that he made it through the night on all sorts of new drips and medicines. Liz and my dad were amazing. Now we think he's got a good chance again.' She tried to fill his mind with hopeful stuff. But it was hard going. 'Hoody, did you hear what I said?'

'Yeah,' he said, without opening his eyes. 'Is it still snowing?'

She glanced out of the window at the soft white flakes. 'Yes. Why?'

'It was minus five degrees centigrade last night,' he said blankly. 'Did you know that?'

'So?' She spoke as gently as she could.

'So Vinny wouldn't live through that,' he

whispered back, eyes still closed. 'That's it. He's dead.'

'No!' She couldn't bear the broken-hearted note in his voice. She would have to tell him now, even if it turned out to be a false trail. 'Steve's seen him!'

The dark eyes flashed open and looked at her. 'When? Where?' If he could have moved, Hoody would have been off the bed and running out of the ward. But the collar contraption kept him strapped in.

'He thinks he has,' she said more cautiously. She told him the exact situation. 'Don't ask me how come Vinny joined the pack instead of going home after the accident,' she said quietly. 'If it is him. And we don't know if he really has turned wild and vicious . . .'

'I don't care, it doesn't matter!' Hoody said, his face eager at the idea that Vinny had survived. 'He isn't dead. That's all I care about! Nothing else matters; only that!'

'We hope.' Now she wished she hadn't said anything. Her first idea had been right. If Steve had made a mistake, Hoody would never forgive her.

But Hoody had made up his mind. He clutched at straws. As far as he was concerned, Vinny was still alive. His eyes burned into her, making her take a step back away from the bed. 'Carly, find him for me!' he pleaded.

They met in the carpark at the back of the supermarket after school – Carly, Cleo and Hanna, together with most of their tutor group. Even Darren was there. The snow and ice was turning to slush, there was a damp drizzle in the air.

'Let's split into small groups,' Hanna suggested. 'We'll cover more ground that way.'

'I reckon we should go off and search for an hour, then come back here and meet up for a progress report,' Cleo said.

Plans were laid: Cleo's group was to stick to the railway line, Hanna's to try the canal. Darren joined a gang that would cover his own estate, and Carly decided to try Beech Hill Park with her group. That way she could call in at the Rescue Centre to let Steve know what they were up to.

'OK?' Hanna was raring to go, convinced

that finding Vinny was only a matter of time. Sooner rather than later they would track down this group of wild dogs, pick him out of the bunch and bring him home.

'Hang on. What do we do if we spot them?' Darren wanted to know. 'Like, Vinny's there and we just say, "Here boy!" and he comes trotting up like a good little doggie! – Not!'

The problem held them up for a few minutes, until Carly came up with an idea. 'If we find him, nobody tries to go near,' she suggested. 'We go to the nearest phone and we ring Steve at my place, tell him exactly where the pack of dogs is. Then he comes along with a proper muzzle and everything.'

'No heroics,' everyone agreed.

They split off with high hopes to comb their areas. Street by street they asked after the pack of dogs, searched down alleyways, near dustbins, in outhouses and garages. Each time they met a shrug and a shake of the head, or a suspicious look.

'This isn't as easy as it looks,' Cleo confessed when the whole group met up an hour later. 'No one we asked had even seen the dogs!'

The others told the same story. 'During the day they just seem to vanish from the estate,' Darren told them. 'It's only at night that people hear them scrabbling in the bins and making a row.'

'Steve says he'll look out for them when he's out in the van.' Carly had called in at home and enlisted his help. Her dad had warned them to be careful. 'They say not to go near if we do find them.'

A few people began to scuff their feet and melt away with excuses like homework or tea. Other stayed for a second attempt, but this time the mood had changed.

'Who'd have thought they could disappear like this?' Hanna said. 'You always see them around when you don't want to.'

'And what if it's a waste of time anyway?' someone else asked. 'We don't know for sure that Vinny's with them.'

A couple more people drifted off.

But Carly stuck with her promise to Hoody. 'Find him for me!' he'd pleaded. He'd never asked her for anything in his life until now.

So she carried on looking, even after the

second attempt had failed and everyone else had packed up and gone home.

'Sorry, Carly,' Cleo said, admitting defeat. They stood at the corner of City Road and Beech Hill. 'We're just gonna have to wait until the dogs decide to show up of their own accord.'

Not good enough, Carly thought. She would take one last look herself; try the park at the back of the centre again. After all, it was one of Vinny's and Hoody's favourite haunts.

So she trudged off through the slush, down the hill towards the park. The streetlamps glared orange, cars queued nose to tail in the homeward rush hour. Their engines chugged out fumes, the people sitting inside stared out with bored expressions.

Then, when she turned in through the park gates, there was a dense wall of darkness and drizzle; no lights, no movement. Here the snow still lay deep, drifted into the hollows and against the walls. It took a while for her eyes to adjust, but now she could make out the swings and roundabouts, the bare flower-beds, the brick sheds for storing gardening equipment.

She reached the long, narrow pond and looked out across the melting ice into silence.

Something caught her attention; dark shapes moving quietly on the opposite bank, the swish of a tail against a bush, the glint of an eye. She waited until she was sure, watched the animals glide between bushes, then out the other side; half a dozen, maybe eight dogs of different sizes, keeping close, trotting to scavenge in a bin by a bench.

At last! Vinny's pack. Carly felt her throat go tight as she tried to swallow. What now? If she left them to run for Steve's help, would they still be here when she came back? She'd promised not to approach. The dogs looked dangerous, with their thin, hungry, scavenging jaws.

The pack moved away from the bin, back to the water. They followed the bank, around the narrow point, heading her way. *Where are you, Vinny?* Carly whispered to herself. She sought out the white chest and tough, stocky build, the curling tail and brown-and-black stripes of Hoody's dog.

Then the pack saw her and stopped short.

They were fifty metres from where she stood. One cut away from the rest and trotted up the snowy slope, a shaggy-haired dog with matted fur and a long, pointed face. He stared down at Carly, growling a warning. She shifted. The growl grew louder.

She knew not to move again. She must wait until the dogs decided what to do, hoping that they wouldn't sense her as a threat but go quietly on their way. 'Vinny?' she whispered again, hoping against hope.

Another dog cut free to join the leader, while the rest stood alert by the water. One yelped, then barked out a deep warning. The main pack milled silently by the pond.

Then she spotted him, his bow-legged walk and barrel chest, his white face and chest. 'Vinny!'

'Vinny, it's me!' She stepped forward. Her advice to the other kids, her father's warning all forgotten. The 'no heroics' message meant nothing now that she'd found him.

Vinny cocked his head to listen, standing stock-still in the middle of the moving pack.

Had he recognised her voice? 'Vinny, here,

boy!' She ignored the snarls of the other dogs, crouched on her haunches and clapped her hands. 'Here, boy! Come here!'

The two dogs on the hill broke into a run. They swept towards her, teeth bared. Carly felt rather than saw them surge down. For a second she closed her eyes. Then they were past her, tails almost brushing her crouching body, one on either side, galloping on across the park, calling the other dogs to follow.

She opened her eyes, breathed again. There was Vinny, still standing in the same place, ears pricked, staring at her without moving a muscle, while the pack ran on.

'Here, boy!' She said it gently, reached out her hand towards him.

The dog lowered his head and took a step forward. His tail had sunk low.

'It's OK, we're not angry with you!' she whispered. 'Come on, come here!'

At last he obeyed. He was thinner, wilder than before, but he still came to Carly's call. Cautiously he put one foot in front of another. While his pack disappeared out of the park, he stayed.

Carly flung out both arms. She was on her knees, hugging him, telling him what a good boy he was, how they'd missed him. 'You're safe now!' she said, holding him tight.

9

They would never know what had made Vinny run away, how long he'd spent looking for Hoody after the accident, how he'd come to join the pack of wandering, wild dogs.

'None of that matters now,' Paul Grey told Carly as they drove to St Mark's. 'He's obviously had a tough time, but it's nothing that a few square meals won't put right.'

Vinny sat in the car at Carly's feet. She'd taken him home to Beech Hill, then they'd sent a message with Steve to Zoe Hood in Beacon Street.

Can you meet us at the hospital? Carly had written. *We'll bring Vinny, but don't tell Hoody anything; just make sure he can see out of the window!*

It would be a surprise. She couldn't wait to see the look on his face.

Vinny seemed to pick up the excited mood. He fidgeted on the journey, raising his head every time the car braked or stopped at lights. Carly patted his head and told him that it wouldn't be long now.

'They won't let a dog into the ward,' Paul Grey warned as they arrived and he found a place in the hospital carpark.

Carly nodded. 'I've fixed something up with Zoe. She should have things ready by now.'

'Do you know which is Hoody's window?' Paul put Vinny on the lead and handed it to Carly. The dog strained to be off.

She nodded and laughed. 'It's as if Vinny knows too!'

He took them towards the hospital building, trotting smartly, tail up, nose twitching. All the lights were lit, the blinds down at the rows of windows in the low-rise block. But one blind was up and the light flooded out on to the pavement.

'That's it!' Carly said, steering Vinny towards it. Her heart was in her mouth as she put her face close to the windowpane and peered inside.

Hoody was out of bed for the first time and sitting in a wheelchair, his back to the window. His neck was now held in place by a different style of collar, until the swelling and bruising finally went down and he could be back to normal. Zoe was in the room with him, tucking a blanket round his legs, trying to get him to comb his spiky hair.

Hoody was mouthing off at her, pushing the comb away, when Zoe looked up and saw Carly. She smiled and winked.

They timed it perfectly. At the moment when Zoe swung Hoody round to face the window, Carly lifted Vinny from the ground and held him in view. They saw each other in the same split second.

Hoody stared. His mouth fell open, he gripped the arms of his wheelchair. Vinny barked and wriggled. He went mad with delight. Then Hoody was grinning and making a thumbs-up signal at Carly. Vinny was squirming free and jumping down, trailing his lead as he dashed along the path towards the main door.

'Oh no!' Carly stood rooted to the spot. 'Come back, Vin!'

Inside the ward, Zoe took over. 'Meet us at the entrance!' she mouthed to Carly and Paul. Then she swung the wheelchair round and rushed Hoody out of the door into the corridor.

They gave chase, following Vinny and calling his name, knowing he would never stop now.

More perfect timing. Zoe got Hoody to the door just as Vinny arrived. They met in the hospital lobby. The dog saw his owner, yelled with pleasure and leaped on to his lap.

Hoody wrapped his arms around him and let him lick his face. He stroked him and held him as if he still couldn't believe he was really there. 'Don't you ever get it into your head to run away again!' he murmured.

'Dad! Liz! Bones is trying to stand up! Come

and look!' Carly rushed out of the laundry room at Beech Hill. She grabbed her father by the arm and dragged him inside.

The donkey struggled to his feet on shaky legs. The rug that was slung over his back to keep him warm slipped sideways and fell to the floor. There he stood, knock-kneed, thin legs wobbling, head too big for his undersized body, still just skin and bone.

But he was getting stronger. The long days and nights of bitter cold were behind him. The vets' care and Carly's loving attention had pulled him through.

'Good lad, well done!' Liz went forward to pat his neck and let him nuzzle at her hand. She smiled at Carly. 'Well done you, too!'

'It's like a miracle,' Carly said quietly. At times she'd lost hope of ever seeing Bones standing on his own feet. But here he was, tottering through the straw towards her, his wounds almost healed, with enough strength to make his own way again.

'There's still a long way to go,' her dad reminded her. 'He'll need plenty of careful feeding – bran, maize and oats twice a day, plus apples and carrots, plus vitamin supplements, plus insulin, plus . . .'

'Stop!' she pleaded. The affectionate little donkey was nudging the palm of her hand, so she dipped into her pocket for a sugar lump. 'A special treat, because you've been so ill,' she warned. 'Don't think you're going to be spoiled like this when you're better!'

Bones snickered gently, then sank to his knees. He'd had enough walking for one day.

So they carried him back on to his bed and made sure that he had plenty of food and water for the morning. Soon it would be time for Carly to go to school. She went upstairs to change.

'Want a lift?' Steve asked when she came back down. 'I'm going to the police station to talk to them about the case against our friend who imports the illegal birds. Your school's on my way there.'

They chatted as they drove, and Carly was glad to hear that the police would probably want to prosecute Mac's owner. 'It'll be a kind of warning to anyone else who wants to copy him,' Steve said. 'It's unlikely that the courts could enforce a stiff sentence, but all the same, people will know they can't get away with it.' He told her that work on the aviary at Sedgewood was going well.

'Oh no!' Carly sat bolt upright as the van pulled up outside school. 'Talking of Sedgewood, today's the big day!' So much had happened in the last twenty-four hours that she'd forgotten that Wednesday was when the whole school voted on the charity money.

She thanked Steve for the lift, and walked reluctantly across the playground. There were people coming up to her and saying well done; they'd heard about Vinny and how she'd rescued him in the end. They crowded round, but she hardly noticed, shrugging it off until her friends came to save her by dragging her into the girls' cloakroom.

'You OK?' Hanna asked, studying her face. 'Carly, what's up?'

'Nothing. When's assembly?' She could hardly think straight.

'In five minutes. Why?'

In five minutes they would know whether Sedgewood had got the money. She would find out if Bones might have the home they wanted.

'I know!' Cleo broke in. 'It's about the city farm.' She held up her hands with all her fingers crossed. 'I've had them like this since I got up!'

So they steeled themselves to go into B Hall and watch the vote, filing in with everyone from their year. The year head came to the front, with the group tutors following behind her. For once, everyone fell quiet.

'As you know, this morning we want you to decide which of three local charities will receive the major donation from our fund-raising efforts,' she announced. Another teacher wrote up the three names on a whiteboard. 'We want you to think very carefully, because obviously each of these organisations does a great job in our community.'

Carly groaned inwardly. A one-in-three chance didn't sound too good for Sedgewood.

'Of course, the two you decide against will stand a chance of receiving money from us in future years, so it's not a once-and-for-all situation.'

Except for the city farm! Carly thought. It

probably wouldn't last another year without extra money.

'I propose to take a vote through a show of hands. Mr Howell, could you count the vote for us, please?'

They got ready. When the first name was called out for a housing for the homeless scheme, a sea of hands seemed to shoot up. Carly closed her eyes while the teacher counted. 'Fifty votes!' he announced as he wrote the figure on the board.

Then again, a second time, in the vote for a kids' activity centre run by volunteers. She held her breath. 'Fifty-seven votes!' Mr Howell said in a loud voice.

'And now, those in favour of giving the money to Sedgewood City Farm!' the year head said.

Carly put up her hand. So did Hanna, so did Cleo. So did everyone in their tutor group who'd joined in the search for Vinny the night before. There seemed to be a lot of hands, all over the hall. But were there enough? Mr Howell counted for what seemed like an age.

'Seventy-two votes!' He wrote the number with a flourish. 'The money goes to Sedgewood City Farm!'

A week later, they had a picture in the local paper of Hoody handing over the giant-sized cheque to Geoff Best in front of the cows and goats who lived at the farm. Vinny sat at their feet, good as gold, while the photographer clicked away.

Hoody had been out of hospital since the weekend, and visiting Bones at Beech Hill every day. Bones's smart, groomed coat and bright eyes made him look like a different donkey from the one Hoody had found tethered by the railway. He was nervous with Bones at first, in case the donkey was scared of him. But Bones seemed to know that Hoody was a friend.

'See, he trusts you.' Carly watched happily as Bones took an apple from Hoody's palm.

'Can I stroke him?'

'Course you can. Look, he wants to say thanks!' She laughed as the donkey nuzzled against Hoody's chest.

Then, on the Monday morning, Carly had been allowed out of school again, this time to help present the cheque.

'I don't want to be in the photograph!' she protested. She was wearing school uniform, which she hated.

So they let her off and made do with Hoody, still wearing a plastic collar, who smiled stiffly at the camera. The journalist from the paper asked Geoff what he proposed to do with the money given by the school.

'It's come at a really good time for us,' he replied. 'The farm has been struggling lately, but this donation will help to see us through until the spring, when we hope to increase the number of visitors. We'll have a new aviary with two macaws, a parakeet and a parrot. And of course, all our usual farm animals, such as cows, goats, sheep and pigs, plus the geese and turkeys you see wandering around the farmyard here.'

The woman reporter nodded and jotted down notes. 'This is great publicity for you. Do you think you might even be able to buy new animals with the money you've been given?'

SKIN AND BONE

Carly pricked up her ears while Geoff Best considered his answer. 'I suppose we might buy in a couple of rare breeds of cows and sheep. Dexter cattle, perhaps. They're Irish, an endangered breed.' He knitted his brows and thought hard. 'Or Gloucester Old Spots, which is a kind of pig you don't see much these days.'

'Or a donkey!' Carly chipped in.

'Great idea,' the journalist agreed. 'That's one thing that's missing round here – a nice friendly donkey. I used to love them when I was a kid.'

'Hmm.' Obviously Geoff hadn't considered it before. 'I suppose there is enough room. I'll have to think about it.'

Hoody caught Carly's eye. 'What's to think about?' he insisted.

He was putting on his tough act for Geoff's benefit, but Carly could see straight through it.

'A donkey can give rides to the kids,' he went on. 'Like on the beach. You could earn a bit of extra money that way, so the donkey wouldn't cost you a penny to keep.'

'Especially if you could get him free,' Carly added.

'From a donkey home,' the reporter suggested.

'Or from us!' She jumped in with both feet. 'We've got one that Hoody rescued. That's how he got hurt. But we managed to bring the donkey into the Rescue Centre in the end. He was seriously ill, but he's getting better now – the donkey, that is. It would be really great if he could come and live here!' Her words tumbled out at first, then ground to a halt. She stared down at her feet, held her breath and waited.

'Great story!' The reporter took it up. She jotted down notes furiously. 'What's this donkey's name?'

They told her all about Bones.

' "Skin and bone" – Bones!' Hoody explained. 'Carly's looking after him at Beech Hill, but he needs a proper home eventually.'

Carly and Hoody stared at Geoff.

'What's the answer?' the reporter asked, pencil poised.

Slowly Geoff scratched his beard, then grinned. 'How can I refuse?'

'That means yes!' Carly jumped into the air and yelled.

The journalist scribbled furiously. 'Can I put it in the article?' she checked. ' "New Home for Abandoned Donkey", that sort of thing?'

'In a week or two, when you're strong enough to be moved, this is where you'll be going!' Carly held up the newspaper photograph for Bones to see.

'He can't understand that!' Hoody scoffed. They were in the park with Vinny, taking Bones for a gentle walk. The snow had gone and snowdrops were poking up through the grass under the trees. They took slow, small steps, leading him on a halter rope.

'Course he can. He understands every word, don't you, Bones?' She showed him the picture of Sedgewood again.

The donkey rolled his eyes and showed his teeth. He blew noisily, nodding his head.

'See!' Carly told him everything – how Geoff Best was making a special stall in the stables for him, along with the ponies, how the geese and turkeys would be able to wander in and out. 'This is it, Bones. This is your five-star donkey hotel!'

Bones opened his mouth. He snatched the photograph from her hands and grasped it between his teeth. Then he chewed and swallowed. In seconds it was gone.

Hoody laughed. 'Yeah! Like, he understands every word!'

Bones chomped happily, while Vinny rolled in the grass. Carly frowned. 'That wasn't meant to happen!'

But then life never went according to plan. A donkey ate the article you wanted for your scrapbook, your friends made fun of you. Tomorrow there would be another accident victim to take care of, another version of Bones to rescue. That was how she liked it to be.

'Come on, then.' She turned the hungry donkey and led him slowly up the hill. 'Let's get you home for tea.'